# THE JOURNAL

# ALSO, BY just Deirdre.

## Short Stories:

Derek and Camella, Homegirl Misled

Samson and Taylor, Cruise Interrupted

Clyde and Ginger, When Love Isn't Enough

Young and Reckless, New Faces

Sought Out, Online Hookup

Pest of a Bug, Work Humor


## Novels:

Something Inside:  Fiction/Suspense

Kallista, The Forbidden One: Fiction/Fantasy/Erotica

# THE JOURNAL

## NANCY BREMEN STORY

*Written by just* Deirdre.

# COPYRIGHT

This is a work of fiction. Names, characters, places, and incidents are either the product of the author's imagination or are used fictitiously, and any resemblance to any actual persons, living or dead, events or locales is entirely coincidental.

Text copyright © 2019 by just Deirdre.
All rights reserved.

No part of this book may be reproduced, or stored in a retrieval system, or transmitted in any form or by any means, electronic, mechanical, photocopying, recording, or otherwise, without express written permission of the publisher.

This is a work of fiction. Names, characters, places, and incidents are either the product of the author's imagination or are used fictitiously, and any resemblance to any actual persons, living or dead, events or locales is entirely coincidental.

Mature audiences only should read this book as its content contains sexual content abuse and violence. Please do not continue reading if you are under the age of 18 or if this content is disturbing to you.

First Edition, Published 2019 by Deirdre Braud
Printed in the United States of America

ISBN-13:978-1-7339521-9-4 Ebook
ISBN-13:978-1-7339521-4-9 Paperback
ISBN-13:978-1-7339521-5-6 Hardcover
Library of Congress Control Number: 2019904117

Cover Design by Naeem Khan
Formatted by Irmalisa

# DEDICATION

For my children, Glynedra, Glynis, Delloid
(Ajamu) Sr. My daughter-in-law, Sharon.
My brother, Demetrius. My significant other, Earl.
My mother, Frankie Mae. Thank you for your
patience endurance and putting up with me as
I was busy writing. Thank you for always being
my biggest crowd, my cheerleaders.
Thank you for believing in me always.

# CONTENTS

# THE JOURNAL
## NANCY BREMEN STORY

# CHAPTER

# 1

ALL MY LIFE, I associated funerals with rainy days. Momma's funeral should not have been on such a sunny day. The irony of that bright, cheery day was not lost on me, even at nine. Birds chirped louder than ever. The sun shone down from her apex. The service passed in a blur of sadness and sheer boredom. When the formalities were over, Grandma Ivie remained seated, so did my twin brother Brian and me.

A tall man with speckled gray hair on both sides of his head ambled towards us. Salt and pepper, Momma called it. Calmly, he kneeled in front of us. In his mid-thirties, he looked about the same age as Momma. He wore a coat, even though it was a little too hot for it. He looked tired, his attire a little shoddy for a funeral. It was as if he'd come from far away and wasn't planning to stay long.

He spoke in a gentle but indifferent tone. "I am sorry for your loss; your momma was a great woman and mother." Then he kissed us both on the forehead and rose to his feet. "Take care of them," he said, avoiding eye contact with Grandma Ivie.

"That's it, Daniel?" she asked, incredulous, her voice raw with emotions. I remember her voice shaking a little as she spoke, the same way Momma's did when she didn't want to break down. "Am I supposed to take care of them? What about you? They just lost their mother, the only parent they had. Don't you have a responsibility here?"

"I can't, even if I want to. I have another life, another family. I can't just show up with two more children out of nowhere." He looked at Grandma for the first time.

"Out of nowhere?" Grandma snapped, throwing her scarf on the ground. *"Out of nowhere?"* She shoved off the chair as though she would charge him right there and then. Her eyes widened with outrage; a fury so powerful that her gaze should have made him burst into flames. I'd never seen Grandma so mad. "They are not just two more children out of nowhere; these are *your* children, Daniel, your firstborns," Grandma hissed between grinding teeth, muffling her anger to avoid the attention of others present at the funeral.

*Our father?* I blinked up at him in confusion.

"I am sorry," he muttered, his tone complementing his expressionless face. Nothing left to say, he walked away.

Grandma's hands shook as her petite frame trembled. "Bastard," she mumbled. Her eyes brimming, she gracefully slipped her handkerchief from her purse and blotted the oncoming tears with a slow dab.

Brian was quiet, more confused than me about all that had happened. The emotional stress from the loss of Momma weighed heavier on him. Shell shocked, he sat slumped in the chair with his head hung low. Shivering, he managed to hold off from making a sound for the better part of a minute. Then he released the most pitiful wail I'd ever heard. Everyone stopped what they were doing and turned toward us.

It frightened me. With dewy eyes, I grabbed Brian and gripped him to my chest, one hand petting his brow as I murmured whatever comfort a nine-year-old could offer. Grandma Ivie rushed over, put her arms around us both, and whispered hoarsely through a tight throat, "Everything will be okay. You will be okay. I'll make sure of it."

Soon Brian quieted. As the stragglers stopped to share their condolences, he kept close to me, focused on the ground.

A man wearing a pair of jeans and a dark suit jacket sat on the empty chair beside us. "I'm Dal, an old friend of your moms from a while back."

I had never seen his face before Momma's funeral. Mixed in with the people I knew, two more of these old friends had come up. I remembered each name as it was told to me: Dal, Ottis, Axel. Old friends, they'd said. I must have nodded but didn't understand.

When Daimhin approached us, Brian and I both jumped up to sandwich him in our hugs. We knew Daimhin; he always had time for us and treated us well. He was a strong man, but his trembling lips that day told me he desperately wanted to cry.

He held us tightly. "Stay strong, kids. And remember, I'm here for you. If either of you ever need anything, call me?" His eyes pleaded as he reached into his pocket for a pen and paper. He jotted his number down on the back of a random business card and gave it to me.

Gazing up at him, I asked, "Anytime?"

"Anytime."

After the funeral, people stopped by the house to pay a visit. They brought cooked meals and envelopes, asked if there was anything needed, anything to help Grandma Ivie. Brian sat on the couch quietly, caught up in a sad world of his own as I longed for our old life and everything about it.

Memories pricked my mind. I disappeared into the basement, home to the packed remnants from our old house. I rummaged through the still-sealed boxes. One labeled Nancy's stuff caught my eye. Ripping off the tape, I yearned to embrace whatever was in the box, things most precious to Momma. Right on top, I found a book with *The Holy Bible* printed in the middle of cover. At the bottom, engraved in silver letters, was the name *Nancy Bremen*.

"But Momma's last name was Hellington." Perhaps it belonged to some unknown namesake of Momma's.

I unfastened the Velcro strip which held the broken lock, opened the book, and flipped through the handwritten pages. I'd never read a Bible, though Grandma Ivie often mentioned events from the Good Book. Even when Brian and I attended church with her, I would sleep for long spells, then wake up whenever Grandma nudged me to sit up straight and pay attention. She was a practicing Christian and did her best to lead us into faith. She often referred to verses from the Bible and would at times narrate the stories from it. At that time, to me, the Bible was a collection of stories with morals, a book with lots of *don'ts* that I didn't like.

Contrary to Grandma, Momma wasn't much into religion, but still she had a Bible. Perhaps a gift from Grandma Ivie or, like the cover said, it belonged to some Nancy Bremen rather than Momma.

I placed the book back in the box and started ravaging through her other things: an old pen, a broken hair clip, a ring. That beautiful ring had a bright red stone, a fine and expensive piece of jewelry, but I didn't remember Momma ever wearing it.

Voices came from the kitchen upstairs. I held the ring tight in my hand and listened. Grandma Ivie asked Brian where I was, and I heard him reply that he hadn't seen me.

"Brea come on; time for supper," Grandma Ivie yelled in her smooth tone.

Supper? I didn't realize I'd been in the basement for quite that long. Once the Bible was safely in Momma's box, I uncrossed my legs and leaped up in a hurried scramble. Taking the steps two at a time, I headed up stairs.

When I opened the door into the kitchen, Grandma Ivie stood there with her hands on her wide hips. "What are you doing down in the basement, Brea?"

"Nothing, looking through Momma's things. What are we going to do with it all?"

"Nothing yet, haven't taken the time to get around to it. You be careful down there; there's stuff all over the place."

"Okay, Grandma, I will." I wanted to ask her about the woman's name on the Bible, which had been tearing at me since I found the book. Uneasy about the question, I decided to go the route of not caring so much. "Who is Nancy Bremen, Grandma?"

"Why, that's your mother," she replied.

"Bremen?"

"Her father, your grandfather, and me, that's our last name. When your mother married your father, her last name changed to his, Hellington, like yours."

A nervous laugh wheezed from me. "How come I never knew your last name was Bremen? I always thought it was the same as ours."

"I don't know, baby; I guess you never noticed."

"So, does this mean you had another name before you got married?"

"Smart girl!" Her praise felt like warm honey on my wounded soul. "Yes, I had a different last name before I married."

"What happened to our grandfather? Where is he now? You never talk about him."

"Brea, your grandfather passed away a long time ago. He was a young man, only forty-one years old. Your momma was about your age then, maybe a few years older," said Grandma Ivie in a shallow voice as her eyes shined with tears. "We can talk another time. Come on; let's eat." She grabbed my hand and led me to the dinner table where Brian sat waiting.

"I'm starving," he grumbled.

"I know, Brian, but we were waiting on your sister."

Brian smirked at me, and I frowned back playfully. I had so many more questions, but seeing how it made Grandma Ivie sad, I decided not to ask her.

***

*Thirteen years old, I'm a teenager! We're teenagers!*

This birthday had me more excited than I had been in a long while. Grandma Ivie, Brian, and I arranged a small birthday celebration. It wasn't much, a few classmates and friends from the neighborhood, but I wished Momma was alive to celebrate with us.

Early that morning, I woke up eager, ready to decorate for our guests. Grandma Ivie was already working in the kitchen by the time I hustled downstairs. She smiled up at me and pulled me into a warm embrace.

"Happy birthday! A teenager, huh?" she said against my head.

I smiled sheepishly. Over the next few hours, we put the finishing touches on the food and the room, then waited for our guests to arrive. The first few guests didn't impress me, girls from school who were not my friends. Even so, they jumped at the invite once I told them Brian and I were having a birthday party.

More people showed than I expected. Right when the party was getting into full swing, I heard a voice I recognized all too well! When Daimhin's low baritone boomed across a room, Brian and I always ran out from whatever rocks we were under. He walked into the living room. I stood in the doorway, receiving the guests, trying to be as nice as possible, just like a grown-up. As Grandma Ivie had said, "You are thirteen now, not a kid anymore."

But on seeing Daimhin, Brian and I scrambled toward him without a care who was watching, just like old times when he came visiting Momma with treats all those years ago. While wooing Momma,

Daimhin had taken us for ice cream in the park and read to us at times before bed. He was always kind to us when Momma was alive, more so now that she was gone.

Daimhin pulled us into a group hug. I snuggled close to him, taking in a whiff of his cologne. I had always liked the way he smelled, soft musk and wood; it was comforting.

"How are my not-so-little ones doing?" he asked when we finally peeled ourselves off him.

"Ew, Daimhin. We're not kids." Brian teased.

"Anyway, I got you 'not-kids' a little something." Daimhin said as he pointed toward two gifts in the doorway. They were big, body size, and covered with sheets. He walked up and stood right between them. With a smile on his face, one hand on each of the gifts, he paused for a moment as we watched in excitement. Then, like a magician performing a trick, he pulled away the sheets. They moved up with a rough swish. Before our eyes sat two electric scooters, a black one and a red one, the latest model, something we never would have bought for ourselves.

Brian and I squealed loudly, eager to go for a ride.

"Black is mine," I shouted.

"Nooooooo," Brian complained. "You get the red one. Black is my favorite color."

Sensing the impending hostilities, Daimhin walked up to me, smiling. He bent and whispered in my ear, "Red is my personal favorite. I got that one for you."

"Ok, I get the red one," I said softly while he playfully winked at me. "Thanks, Daimhin." I hugged him again.

"Yeah, thanks, Daimhin. I'm going outside to go ride this." Brian walked away from the two of us.

"Where's your grandma, dear?" Daimhin asked, turning toward me.

"I guess she's in the kitchen."

"All right. I need to go say hi." He gave me another hug before he went to find her.

I smiled as I watched him walk toward the kitchen, then I joined the other guests at the party. Walking through the hallway, it felt great seeing all these people here. The last time we had so many visitors was the funeral.

While our guests talked, laughed, and enjoyed sodas and birthday cake, I heard girls giggling, hyperexcited, in the other room. They stared at Brian as he fooled around with his scooter. The way they ogled him all dreamy-eyed, I realized why all these girls had come to this party despite not being actual friends of mine. They rolled the tips of their hair around their fingers and flashed bashful half-smiles when he glanced their way.

I had to admit, my brother was a cute boy, with his curly black hair and olive complexion. He had sparkling white teeth that gleamed when he smiled, even though he didn't do enough to keep them that way.

The girls kept drooling over him, but Brian was busy riding his scooter, one with the wind. I watched him, glad to see him out of his room, happy for once. And for a split second, I saw what they all saw: happy, carefree Brian, young and bold and growing strong.

Once our classmates left, Daimhin called for us to say his goodbyes.

I clasped my arms around his waist; I always hated when he had to go. "Will you be back to visit soon?"

Daimhin chuckled, soft and kind, amused by my enthusiasm. "Maybe in another month. There is a lot going on at work, but if you need me, I'm just a phone call away." He kissed me on top of the head. On his way out, he gave Brian's shoulder a gentle squeeze and told him to be careful with the new ride. "And make sure you always wear your helmet."

With that our last guest left the house. Moments later, Grandma popped in with a garbage bag, ready to clean up.

I got up and stacked a few cups and plates together.

Grandma Ivie shooed me away. "It's your birthday. Go have fun. I'll clean up."

"You sure?" I asked, dropping some disposable cups into the bag.

"Yes, sweetie. Now get going." She swatted me with the napkin in her hands as though I were a fly pestering her.

I slinked off to my room, took out a book from my bookshelf, and opened it to where I'd left off. Investigative fiction was an addiction, my second favorite pastime after watching crime procedurals on TV.

AT SIXTEEN, BRIAN and I were high school seniors. For the long years since Momma passed, Grandma Ivie acted as the mother we didn't have. In her early sixties, she dedicated all her time and energy to raising us. I couldn't remember her ever taking a day off from her chores. Grandma always said that medication wasn't for her; I didn't blame her since she hardly ever needed it. She did her own laundry and drove for herself. Quite the spring chicken, she raised two teenagers all by herself. But she was only able to do so much.

Brian and I helped however we could. A lot of kids our age gave their parents grief, but I liked to think we were different. We hardly ever gave

Grandma Ivie problems. Possibly we felt so well cared for or we were exemplary kids. Or we knew how much strain we put on Grandma Ivie without acting out.

For two kids so much alike, Brian and I had grown so far apart over the years. I was active in track, basketball, and volleyball. After school I worked out. I liked boys but didn't date much and never got involved with anyone intimately. I didn't know for sure why that was, but it was my way.

Probably because I didn't see many men around growing up. I didn't have a father, and though Daimhin cared for us, he never stayed. Then there was my baby brother, an introvert with emotions bigger than he could contain.

The opposite of me, Brian didn't take part in any sports, didn't hang out with friends, or indulge any hobbies. Some kids teased him, as if shyness made him weak, which in Brian's case was far from the truth. I'd long expected his timid reserve to be temporary, a part of his mourning. I just knew that he'd return to himself as we progressed in school.

In the meantime, every bit the big sister, I mother-henned him, which sometimes didn't work so well. Lately he had become even more shy, quiet, and private. Since he wouldn't talk to me about it, I spied on him at school. That first morning passed without event. At lunch, Toby

Wyatt, one of the star basketball players, threw balls of paper at the back of Brian's head. Sitting alone at the lunch table, Brian didn't move. He held onto his backpack tightly and stared at the table, despite the balls hitting him.

No one moved to stop Toby; not a single person even looked in his direction. The other guys with Toby laughed as he continued to taunt my brother.

My blood boiled.

Slamming my bag on the floor, I rushed toward Toby without thinking, propelled by my anger. I kicked him in the stomach. Caught off guard, Toby sank down to his knees with pain on his face. Though at heart I was a little scared that Toby might fight back, I wasn't done yet. I grabbed the nearest carton of milk and flung it at him. It hit him square in his temple and spilled down the side of his face.

"Leave him alone!" I could have heard a pin drop as Toby turned my way. With a glare sharp enough to cut glass, I told him, "I will not let you bother my brother like that. Don't you dare touch him ever again!" I made my way to Brian.

Toby stared with wide eyes. I expected the bully to charge me or at least yell. He didn't do any of that. Instead Toby was surprised. Bullies never expect anyone to stand up to them.

I walked to Brian, got him up from his chair, and walked him to the door. He stayed quiet all the way out of the cafeteria. I led him to the practice field, and he followed like a lamb. We settled on one of the bleachers, and still Brian wouldn't say a word.

At this point I was vexed with Brian too. How did he let this happen to him and just stay quiet about it? "How long has this been going on?" I asked, afraid he would refuse to answer me.

"A while," he finally said.

"How long is *a while*?"

"It's been going on for about two years now. Nothing serious. Just the usual talk and an occasional shove."

*Two years?* He just said *two years*, and no one knew about it.

"Why didn't you tell anyone? Why didn't you tell Grandma? Or me? Or Daimhin?"

"I didn't want you guys worrying. Or doing something stupid. Like pissing Toby off. Seriously, do you know how much trouble you just created for me?"

I huffed at that. "I didn't get you into any trouble; I just saved you. Bullies only bully people when they know no one will stand up to them. You should have punched that idiot ages ago."

Brian got to his feet and shook his head. "I'm hoping for both our sakes that's true. Because if it isn't, you just got me into a lot of trouble." He stalked off.

I didn't see Brian or Toby for the rest of the day. Hours later, when I was back home and settled in front of the TV watching a crime investigator process evidence, Brian slipped in through the side door. Not wanting to scare Grandma Ivie, I didn't ask him why he had disappeared. The last thing I wanted was for her to get worked up about Brian being bullied. It was in everyone's favor to be quiet.

Or so I thought.

About a week before Grandma Ivie's 66th birthday, Brian rushed past me in the school hallway. When I saw his flustered scowl, I ran after him, calling out his name, but he didn't reply or slow down. He walked straight into the men's toilet. Ten minutes passed before he came out of the restroom.

He glared at me from red-rimmed eyes.

"What happened, Bri?"

"Nothing. I'm all right." He walked on as though I hadn't been waiting for him by the door.

I trudged after him. "Wait up. You're not all right. You've been crying."

"Yeah, why not just use the public address system, since you're hellbent on letting the entire world know!" he snapped. "Just leave me alone, Brea."

I stopped in my tracks. Brian never spoke to me like this, not even when he was mad at me. The entire day, even when we got home, he was brusque, replying to everyone in monotones. While Brian was the quiet one, he was never this quiet and never so rude.

I was hoping Grandma would notice, but if she had, she didn't let on.

Friday, the day before Grandma's birthday, all hell broke loose for Brian. I searched for him after classes, but he was nowhere to be found. When he finally came home, his shirt was rumpled and torn; he had a cut right above his eye. Through the blood seeping around his eye, Brian glared at me as though I had busted his eye myself.

"Brian! What happened?"

"This is what happens when you meddle in other people's business. I told you it would backfire! I told you! Now look what he did. Next time just mind your business!" He then stomped off to his room.

It took a while for his words to register in my mind, to understand what he had been going on about. Toby had done that to him. I stalked off to

Grandma's room without thinking of Brian's warning. I told her everything I knew, and together, we went to his door. Grandma Ivie knocked lightly at first but a little firmer when he didn't open. Finally, she opened the door and walked in with me in tow. To my surprise, his room was a mess. The bed wasn't made, pillows scattered on the floor like dry leaves. Shoes lay upside-down beside socks rolled in the shape of cotton balls on his bookshelf. A discomforting stench permeated the room. This was so unlike Brian, who was organized and scrupulous even when he was small.

Brian sat on his study chair in a corner, staring out into the dark. He had done a piss-poor job of cleaning the wound, as it was still bleeding.

"Brian?" Grandma Ivie whispered.

Brian looked past her to glare at me. "Can't you just mind your own business? Get out of my room!"

I didn't move until Grandma nodded at me. That night, she cleaned his wound and suggested he speak with the authorities. He refused, adamant that he didn't want anyone making things worse for him. Again. He insisted he could handle it by himself, but we all knew that wasn't going to happen.

In the kitchen Grandma Ivie told me, "Daimhin will be over tomorrow. I think he might listen if Daimhin speaks to him. What's this bully's name?"

"Toby. Toby Wyatt." I sighed, angry at him and at my brother.

"All right. I hope Daimhin can talk some sense into him about this Toby character."

I was on edge all night, tossing and turning, worrying about Brian. Morning brought Daimhin's bright smile. I tried my hardest to resist eavesdropping as he and Brian spoke on the porch. When a TV commercial came on, I had nothing to distract me, so I tiptoed toward the window.

"You shouldn't be mad at her for wanting to help, Brian," Daimhin said. "That's all she was trying to do."

"Look how that went," Brian muttered.

"I'm sure she meant no harm." Daimhin replied, and the two of them sat in silence for the next few minutes. "You know, a crazy thought just popped into my head. What do you plan to do after high school?"

"Well, I haven't thought about it." Brian sounded spent.

"I think you should train up and go into the Navy, just like I did."

He let out a nervous laugh. "I would never. I'm not Navy material."

"Oh, come on. Think about it. You'll love the sea. Think about how much you'll be doing, the opportunities this would present to you. You'll already be training up to defend yourself from this Toby guy. And by the time you're seventeen, you can apply to join the academy."

"Why would I want to do that?"

"I never regretted joining the Navy. Not only do you get to serve your country, there's a ton of other stuff you benefit from. I've been a better person since I joined. I learned discipline and commitment in the best conceivable way. It's all up to you though. No pressure but promise you'll think about it."

"I promise."

Those words brought a smile to my lips. Brian hardly ever spoke, so when he did, he meant it.

While I'd tried to adjust as best as I could to Momma's death, Brian made no such effort. He wasn't one to associate with many people naturally, and after Momma's passing, he seemed even more determined to battle his demons himself.

Momma must have expected it, for on her deathbed, she said to him, "Reach out to Daimhin if you ever need advice or help or just somebody to talk to. He's an honorable man."

And now Daimhin saved the day. Brian started martial arts classes that same week.

***

Brian and I drifted further apart after graduating high school. He enlisted in the Navy. Though he always wanted a college education, he was determined to become a naval officer. Daimhin's talk with him played a huge part in that decision.

After registration, Brian headed out to bootcamp at the recruit training command in Great Lakes, Illinois. Along with his practical training, he took classes in seamanship and basic academics. From there, he moved on to Newport, Rhode Island, to begin Officer Candidate School for twelve weeks. At OCS, he continued to train on his journey towards becoming a Navy line officer.

All that kept Brian absent from home for a significant period.

Grandma Ivie and I wore long faces for a while. While we wished him the best in life and supported all the dreams he had, we felt left out since he didn't discuss his plans. I didn't mention to Grandma that I'd heard Daimhin talking to him about it a couple of years prior. Still, we often discussed his progressing career, and smiles would break out on both our faces.

I was quite proud. He was finally moving forward in life after Momma's death.

Once Brian left home, I found myself brooding from time to time. I couldn't help but feel apprehensive about the distance between us. He seldom called and visited even less. I took comfort in the news that his classes and training were going well, that he was looking forward to starting his officer training.

But I missed him.

After high school, I attended college. I obtained my bachelor's degree in criminal justice, and for my master's degree, I majored in forensic science with an emphasis on biology. My keen interest in law enforcement weighed heavily into that decision. I held out hope of joining the FBI.

When I explained my plans to Grandma, she wasn't the least bit surprised. "Well, I always kind of figured you'd go that route. You always loved those crime programs."

Torn between being out in the field in the thick of things and working in a lab analyzing evidence, I knew I'd make an excellent FBI field agent, but the Criminal Investigation Division, which oversees FBI investigations, also appealed to me. Both positions fit me, so I straddled the fence and applied for both, hoping to be picked for one.

But I leaned toward lab analyst.

If I went for the agent position, I'd have to leave Grandma Ivie home alone for the twenty-one weeks of training in Quantico, Virginia. Though I was sure Grandma would insist that I go, I still felt guilty at that idea.

I hoped that if I was able to work with the FBI, I would remain based in Virginia. And with that hope in mind, I studied diligently, day and night. When I was not in class, I was usually at the gym where I picked up a new sport, boxing.

The first few weeks of training were the worst. I wondered if my trainer, Jake, ever thought of dumping me. I had zero boxing skills and a weak fist. Worse still, I was out of breath in no time.

"Breathe as you punch!" Jake would yell as I punched the pads he held. "Don't hold that breath! Come on!"

I still held my breath and felt like I'd pass out. Without air I soon couldn't power my punches anymore.

However, Jake persevered.

I genuinely loved boxing. Nothing compared to the rush. Every jab and every punch brought me a thrill that often left me beaming like a star-struck lover. Boxing was exhilarating, a surefire way to get the blood flowing and the heart pumping. Besides being exceptionally good at the sport, I found it to be great at stress busting. I could clear my thoughts, seek solace in the bag; it was therapy for me. No matter if I were sad, happy, angry, or just bored, I took it to the bag and worked out whatever emotion I was feeling.

As I gained skill, I began to carry myself with a great deal of confidence. I walked with my head high and shoulders straight, and my determined posture intimidated most men into respecting my disinterest in dating. Physically, people were already inclined to stare at me. I took after Momma, a very slender, athletic young lady with a dark complexion and striking features. However, where she was a short woman, I was nothing of the sort. I stood at 5'9, a few inches shy of Brian.

I loved hearing others remind me that I looked exactly like her because she was more than just beautiful. She had the most gorgeous pixie face with the softest skin. I often caressed her face, running the back of my hand ever so gently along the contours of her cheek, and she would pet me in the same fashion. We would put our foreheads together and grin.

Oh, how I loved my momma and how I missed her.

# CHAPTER

# 3

ONCE THE FORMALITIES of my college graduation were over, Grandma Ivie, Brian, Daimhin, and I went out for a celebratory gourmet dinner. The waiters loaded the table with rich, spicy dishes and bottles of bubbly champagne. Sweet, savory aromas wafted up my nostrils as I settled in with my family to celebrate that day.

"What's your plan now that college is done?" asked Daimhin, leaning toward me with wide, interested eyes that practically bore into me.

Between mouthfuls of chicken, I said, "I applied to the FBI a couple of months ago, and we'll have to see how that goes. In the meantime, I'm still teaching at the gym. I'll continue living with Grandma Ivie, helping with bills and everything. Like a real adult. Let's see… What else? Hmm, I think that's all for now. I'm free to explore the world and live my life now that I'm finished with college!"

Brian nodded and with a mischievous grin, said, "Even freedom ain't free."

All of us at the table chuckled at the familiar saying, and then I jerked a thumb toward Brian. "As for my dear brother here, he completed his college classes and officer training two years ago but didn't bother to tell any of us so we could be there to show our love and support. He now ever so casually informs us that he has decided to make a career of the Navy, meaning we will see even less of him."

"Yeah, about that, Brian…" Daimhin grunted. "Why didn't you let any of us know about your graduation ceremony?"

I stealthily glanced at Brian out of the corner of my eye, eager to hear his explanation.

Brian shifted in his seat. "Well… Daimhin… Things were happening at breakneck speed back then, and before I knew it, I was done. I didn't give it a second thought, and I didn't want you to rearrange your schedules and book flights for Rhode Island at such short notice."

"Oh please, Brian, find a better excuse!" I groused. "You know we would all have arranged to be there. That was a huge accomplishment, so why would you for one moment think we wouldn't want to be there?"

While Brian tried to hide the fact that he was blushing, Grandma Ivie added, "I would have loved to be there too, Brian. You know I love you to the moon and back."

"Yeah, and maybe there is something you don't want us to know about? A new girlfriend? A boyfriend, maybe?" I commented with a wry smile. "What are you hiding, Brian? You sure are a secretive lil brother."

Brian looked over at me and stared straight into my eyes. "Just because you're a few minutes older doesn't make me your little brother, Brea. And just so you know, my business is just that. My business." He let me off the hook and turned to the others at the table. "I want to apologize anyway, Grandma Ivie and Daimhin, for not inviting you to my graduation."

Leaning over and nudging Brian with an elbow, Daimhin replied, "It's okay. It was a big moment for you, and I know Nancy would have been so proud."

I still felt the need to tease him. "Ah, wow, an apology for Grandma and Daimhin but none for me. So cool."

"Oh, Brea, leave your brother alone. I'm sure he has his reasons!" chided Grandma Ivie.

Brian was a different person than he had been just a few years ago. In the past, I had beaten up on him without any reaction, but the timid boy I was used to was gone. In his place was a buff, tough man, but I wasn't privy to whatever events had changed him so extensively.

"How was the training? What all have you learned?" I asked. "Teach me a thing or two."

"And why would I do that?" Brian retorted playfully.

"It may come in handy someday. C'mon, Bri, help me save someone's life. Or my own. You would be so proud, wouldn't you?"

"Sometimes, to save lives, you must take lives." Brian's words had a finality that sucked the air from my lungs.

Everyone fell quiet. Sensing the unease in that silence, Daimhin turned to Grandma Ivie. "Speaking of taking lives, have you been keeping up with the news lately?"

My grandmother nodded. "Whenever I get the chance. But there's just so much violence and tragedy, it can be painful to keep up. Why? What have you heard?"

"There have been multiple killings across different states within the past two years, the victims all males in their early twenties. The news guy said that it may be a serial killer, but they have no suspects or leads. The authorities are trying to find any connections or motives." He gave Brian his patented meaningful stare. "Be careful, son; the victims were all around your age. Be mindful of your whereabouts and surroundings."

Brian acknowledged the statement by nodding rapidly before scooting his chair out and excusing himself.

I said, "Well, I, for one, am thinking about taking shooting lessons, getting myself a permit, and buying a small handgun. A girl can't be too cautious."

"For real, Brea?" Grandma Ivie blurted out. "That's plain crazy."

"It's a crazy world, Grandma."

"I think it's okay for her to get a pistol," Daimhin chimed in.

All my life he always knew what I wanted and supported me whenever I needed help. He acted as a father, mother, and sincere friend all wrapped up in one. Thinking on this I watched Daimhin sip lemonade from his glass. I leaned a bit toward him to get a whiff of his fragrance, wood and clay. *This man is God sent.*

"Is everyone done with dinner, ready to go?" he asked as Brian came back. "I have a surprise for Brea."

I glanced at Grandma, clueless but excited. Both Grandma and I turned to Daimhin and nodded.

"All right. let's head out." He motioned for the check and went ahead to settle the bill.

As we exited the restaurant, a sleek Infiniti sports car pulled up and stopped a few feet ahead of us. A young man, dressed sharply in a freshly pressed valet uniform, climbed out of the glittering red vehicle and walked toward us.

I glanced back to see who owned the ritzy car.

Nobody. We were the only people waiting.

I wondered what that guy was thinking; that wasn't our car. The valet walked straight up to me and handed me the keys. Dumbfounded, I let the keys slip into my palm as I gaped at him in disbelief. Without a word, he spun on his heel and returned to the car. Opening the driver door, he gestured for me to climb in.

I managed to find my voice. "Sir, I think there's been a mistake."

The man took a folded piece of paper from his jacket lapel. "Brea Hellington?" he asked, looking directly at me.

"Yes," I murmured.

He read, "Happy graduation from Mr. Moderze."

Brian and I turned to Daimhin, wide eyed with surprise, and Grandma Ivie gasped behind me.

He chuckled as if embarrassed. "Hope you don't mind, but I couldn't let you keep driving that rusty old death trap of yours."

I ran toward Daimhin and hugged him tightly as I cried with joy. I continued saying, "Thank you, thank you, thank you!"

Daimhin returned my hug, trying to keep a modest smile. "Happy graduation, Brea. You deserve something nice. On that note, I will be heading home. Work tomorrow." He wrapped his arm around my shoulders. "Good seeing you again. Take care of yourself." He then walked over to Grandma Ivie and draped his arms around her without exerting too much force, as if he were afraid to hurt her. When he was done, he doubled back to Brian and extended his hand.

Brian grabbed his hand and gave a firm handshake. "Thank you for being here for us."

"Always. Stay connected, Brian. Let me know how things are going with your military training." He swung around one last time to me to give me another hug. "Drive safe, and all the paperwork is in the glove compartment."

The valet brought over Daimhin's car, and as he drove off, we all waved goodbye.

"Dang! A spanking new Infiniti!" Brian exclaimed. "Brea, can I drive?"

"Never!" I replied, sticking out my tongue.

"Well, I might not have a gift for you," Brian said as he reached for my purse. "Or one from Daimhin, but I can take this from you." He took out my key chain, a profile of the Eiffel Tower, that served as a bookmark more often than not.

"You can't take that, Brian. It's the only one I have."

"Well, we'll get you another one. I need a tiny keepsake from you. And hey, you at least have a car."

Now that he put it that way, my heart softened. "Fine, fine. I love you too." Just after I spoke, I heard a sob from beside me, and I turned to see Grandma Ivie wiping away her tears. "C'mon, Grandma, it's a happy thing!"

"That was very generous of Daimhin, Brea. I wish Nancy were alive to witness this day."

"Grandma Ivie, please don't cry. Brian and I, we both still have you, and you have done a wonderful job in raising us! Now, let's all get into the car and go home. It's been a long day."

The drive back home was filled with random conversation and laughter. I enjoyed the smooth handling of the Infiniti. From bumper to bumper, the car was a beauty. I admired each one of its stunning details. The flawless red paint shone just as bright as the blazing sun above, which was beaming off the hood and into the supple leather interior. The front panel was elegant and compact with a matte black dashboard, a quality sound system, and a fully automated air conditioner.

The car smelled of authentic leather, the best fragrance ever. Well, not the best, but among the best. I liked wood and clay better.

Brian leaned between the seats. "Guess what? I'm leaving the Navy and moving into this car."

"Over my dead body," I snapped.

He only giggled in reply.

While parking the car in the garage, I was extra cautious. While Brian and Grandma rushed into the house, I stopped at the stairs to have another glance of that beauty, which I still didn't believe was mine. Looking at that mean machine, I was able see my reflection in the shiny, metallic rims; each surrounded by rugged, gravel-encrusted tires.

Once inside, I noticed the message light blinking on the home phone. Grandma Ivie pressed the play button. The Federal Bureau of Investigation wanted to schedule a time for me to come in for an interview! My gut tightened when I heard the words *a forensics position in the Criminal Investigation Division.*

My absolute dream job hung within my grasp.

As the message played, I froze where I stood. I blinked, unsure if I was dreaming. In a few moments my incredulity faded, unleashing my excitement. Unable to restrain myself, I jumped up and down with a squeal. Brian had been busy flipping through the TV channels. He got up from the sofa and turned to me, grinning. I ran toward him and, from a yard away, jumped into his hug. He caught me like a baby, my arms around his neck and my legs encircling his waist.

"Oh my God, Bri, do you know how much I wanted this?" I shouted.

He shrugged in reply.

"That's all you have ever talked about," said Grandma Ivie with a soft smile.

The last time I'd hugged Brian so passionately was at Momma's funeral. I loosened my grip on him, and he put me down. Still lightheaded, I rushed upstairs for pen and paper so that I could write down the contact name and number. I'd respond to the call first thing in the morning.

Dancing up the stairs toward my bedroom, I skipped up two steps, then back down one, snapping my fingers and humming. I yelled over my shoulder, "Call me Federal Agent Hellington." I flung my head back, letting my hair swing free around my face as I grinned cheekily. Pen and notebook in hand, I ran all the way down the stairs and jotted down the number.

It was the perfect ending to a perfect day; all that was left was my nightly ritual.

Once upstairs and in my bedroom, I shut the door and went into the bathroom to run myself a shower. I lathered up, grinning, all the while thinking about the genuine possibility of becoming an FBI agent. I had filled my childhood with a passion for investigative shows and detective stories. Now here I was, one step closer.

When I turned on the shower radio, one of my favorite Earth Wind and Fire songs, *Let's Groove Tonight*, was playing. Standing on my tiptoes, I sang along, "Oh yeah, let's groove tonight," and snapped my fingers. I put a little dip into my moves, bounced up and down, and ever so slightly swayed to the beat, as I continued to lather my body all over with the luxuriously silky feel of the shower wash. As I rinsed away the suds, I savored the warm water streaming over my face, then down my body, until the soap circled its way down the drain. I stood in the spray for a bit longer, staring at nothing, simply enjoying the moment.

The radio announcer's husky voice shook me out of my trance, and I reached to turn off the taps. When I stepped out of the shower, the cool breeze caressed my wet skin, sending chills up my spine. I grabbed the fluffy bath towel off its hook and wrapped it snugly around my body. At the washbasin I stooped slightly to take my body moisturizing balm from the bottom of the cabinet above it. I liked to smooth it on my skin while I was still damp to lock in the moisture and keep my skin soft and smooth.

Still my mother's daughter.

I let the towel drop to the bathroom floor. Standing naked before the now fogged mirror, I twisted the cap open and poured a dime-sized dollop into my hand. I inhaled deeply the enticing apple-cucumber scent. Once I'd finished moisturizing, I picked up my towel, put it back on the hook, and slipped into my favorite silky nightgown. Its smooth softness brushed against my skin, and I sighed deeply.

Out in my dimly lit bedroom, the laptop screen light shone brightly. I decided to sit down and jot down a few things for the FBI interview. I needed to prepare; I didn't want anything standing between me and this position.

"I am tough, I am smart, and I am ready," I told myself repeatedly.

Once I was done researching the Forensics Analyst position for the night, I snapped the laptop lid shut and climbed into bed.

I'd never been this happy.

CHAPTER

# 4

I DROVE UP the highway in my new sedan, my hands gripping the wheel tightly. So many times I'd visualized driving to the FBI Academy headquarters. Now that it was finally happening, I still couldn't believe it. I had read everything about the FBI and double-checked all my paperwork, so I was confident. Still, there was a knot in the pit of my stomach and a slight dryness in my mouth.

I had a sense of the questions I would be asked, and while I went over them in the car, I felt like a bit of a clown talking aloud to myself. But since I wanted the interview to be perfect, I kept practicing. I would typically have my radio on, allowing the rich sound from the surround-sound speakers to bounce around the car, but on that drive, I kept it off. I wanted it to be peaceful so that I remained focus as I rehearsed my answers.

After about two hours of driving and rehearsing, I finally stood outside the academy. My mouth dropped open in awe. I had expected to be wowed by the facility, but my mind wasn't prepared for the beauty my eyes beheld. The beige building stood tall, overpowering everything around it. The imposing black sign, which read Federal Bureau of Investigation Academy, stared back at me. The lush green lawns surrounding the façade added to its serenity and grandeur.

Well, not so much serenity for me at that moment. Standing before the entrance, my knees wobbled. Dry as the California desert, I swallowed a few times. I stifled an urge to turn around and drive away. This interview meant a lot to my future, and I didn't know if I had the strength for it. Struggling to muster my courage, I inwardly chided myself, *Get it together, girl. This is what you have worked so hard to achieve. You CAN do this; you WILL do this. Now go in there and grab hold of this position.*

Perspiring and shaky, in a daze, I momentarily closed my eyes to let the feeling pass. I took a couple of deep breaths. When I felt calmer, I straightened my shoulders, headed toward the revolving door, and walked straight over to the gentleman at the front desk to check in.

"Hello, my name is Brea Hellington. I have an appointment this morning with—"

"Can I see your identification please?" He gave me a bored blink and a cardboard smile.

"Sure." I opened my purse and retrieved my driver's license. "Here you go." I handed it to him.

He wrote the necessary details in his logbook and handed it back to me. Gesturing across the room, he said, "Please take a seat over there. Someone will be down to fetch you shortly."

I turned to the area he indicated and spotted an empty chair. My casual gait forced, I walked over to the chair, sat down, and reviewed my notes in my head again. With my level of preparation, I assured myself, that position was mine.

I didn't have to wait long.

Heels clicked against the marble floor and stopped a foot from where I was sitting. I looked up to find a mature woman appraising me. Brows furrowed she had a stern, cold expression. Her suit was custom fitted and neatly pressed. From her unenthusiastic stare, I imagined she was the type that interacted with people only out of necessity.

When she had my attention, she asked, "Ms. Hellington?"

"Yes, I'm Brea Hellington."

She extended her hand. I extended mine. When our palms locked briefly, I found that she had the firmest handshake of any woman I had ever met.

"I'm Mattie Dyer. We spoke on the phone a few days back. I will be interviewing you today."

"Nice to meet you, Mattie," I replied, sounding more confident than I felt on the inside.

"Agent Dyer, please. I'd rather keep this professional."

"Sure, um, sorry, Agent Dyer." I replied, wishing for the ground to swallow me alive. It hadn't been five minutes, and I was already goofing up.

Agent Dyer led the way to the elevators. As I followed her, I almost asked her if I had ruined everything and if we could start over. I managed to remain calm and keep my mouth shut all the way up to level 14. When we stepped from the elevator, I took in my surroundings to keep from rambling nervously. Agent Dyer and I passed through so many security precautions that I lost count.

All around me, people held their ID tags raised for the many checkpoints that strategically divided the building. The different textures of innumerable voices melded into a background hum as people greeted each other and asked questions. Their quick footsteps came and went as they bustled about their duties. I liked the buzz of it all, but I reminded myself to keep my cool because I would soon be working there with all these people.

When we walked into Agent Dyer's office, the chilly blast of her extra-cold air conditioning made me shiver slightly. She shut the door and gestured to the single guest chair. After I sat down, she seated herself in her large leather chair behind her large mahogany desk. Right behind her, hanging on the wall, were a couple of framed certificates.

Personally, I never liked people flaunting their professional credentials or academic achievements like trophies. I prefer to let my work speak for me. People would learn who I was, irrespective of what was hanging on the wall. *I won't do that in my office*, I decided.

"Why do you want to work for the FBI?" Mattie Dyer asked, leaning back in her chair. Clearly, she wasn't the type to waste time with formalities.

I lowered my gaze from her certificates to her. Despite cutting an imposing figure, the formality of calling her Agent Dyer didn't fit the stern woman. Mattie seemed more appropriate for a woman with a loose bun and barely-there makeup. Maybe that was because she had introduced herself as Mattie on the phone. I decided to call her Mattie in my head and hoped it wouldn't slip through when I spoke.

I cleared my throat. "I've always believed, without law enforcement, America would not be what it is. The principles that hold this country in place would be mere words if criminals could run freely. In this vein, I want to work here because I want to actively make America a safer, better place."

It wasn't clear whether my short speech impressed Mattie. For a moment, I wondered if she considered my words cliché, but as far as I knew, speaking a clichéd truth was better than uttering unique lies.

"But there are other ways to make America safe," Mattie said quietly. "There are several other agencies you could have applied to. Why the FBI specifically?" She seemed unimpressed. I should have thought of a better answer, but it was too late.

"Because it's the pinnacle of law enforcement in America. It's the highest authority on home soil and addresses the offenses that affect the country the most: organized crime, white collar offenses, cyber-security, counterintelligence, and terrorism. No other law enforcement agency affects the safety of Americans on such a large scale."

Mattie blinked with a nod so slight that I almost didn't catch it. Because of her blank expression, I wasn't sure if it was a nod of approval or not.

She asked many other questions, and despite my research, they became increasingly more difficult. My confidence plummeted. Tempted to make things up, I remembered what Daimhin once said, "Best thing with the truth is you don't have to remember what you said." So, I spoke the truth. Genuine, direct, and unadulterated. In retrospect, many of my answers seemed vague, incomplete, or plain stupid, but I answered honestly and earnestly.

At the end of the interview, which took an eternity, Mattie looked straight into my eyes: "Why should I choose you?" Her gaze read my every micro expression. "Of all the candidates, why should I choose you, Miss Brea? Convince me."

After everything I imagined and rehearsed for this interview, nothing went as planned. This unexpected question knocked the breath from me. "Plans are the first casualty of any operation," Daimhin once said when we had to cancel a fishing trip due to rain.

Strange, whenever I was stuck, Daimhin came to the rescue.

I couldn't think of any words to convince Mattie. My palms grew wet, and a drop of sweat slid from my nape and down my spine before being absorbed in my white silk shirt, which I bought just yesterday for this interview. I held onto my bag, trying to gather every bit of confidence left in me.

Mattie waited for my answer with a plain face and uninterested eyes.

How would I answer if Daimhin had asked this question?

"Agent Dyer, I don't know all the answers, at times I have none of them," I heard myself say, "but I assure you, if you ask me a question that I don't know the answer to, I have the energy, commitment, and perseverance to leave no stone on the goddamn earth unturned to find you the answer. I will get that answer for you, no matter what. And that's what makes me different: I never give up on answers." For the first time, in more than an hour sitting together, I saw a glimmer in her otherwise dull eyes.

When the oral interview was over, Mattie walked me to a nearby room and handed me papers for skill assessments. I had shown my interest in becoming a forensic examiner, and the questions assessed my aptitude for that position.

In the quiet room, the grind of my pencil on the paper seemed as loud as a power drill. I knew my mind was overreacting, so I focused on answering the questions while my mind replayed my performance during the interview.

Two hours later, after I had finished all my tests, Mattie took the papers and said,

"Congratulations. Of course, we'll have to see what you wrote in there."

"Thank you for having me," I told her, adding to myself, *If I must go down, I'll at least crash with grace.*

She walked me to the elevators and then to the first-floor lobby, where she informed me that she would contact me between two weeks and a month, after all my assessments, background checks, and history reports had been processed.

"See you around... Maybe."

I nodded and said, "Have a momentous day."

Relieved, I walked out the revolving doors and headed back to where I'd parked my car. Before I started the engine, I quickly reviewed the interview. The bad parts stuck out in my mind. But then I consoled myself: I remained calm for the oral section and spoke truthfully, if not always smartly. While the written assessment had been tough, the material felt familiar.

I sighed as I realized I might have to wait a whole month to hear any news; I hoped not to have a heart attack from the anticipation. Finally, I started up the car. With a last glance at the magnificent building, I prayed to see this place again. With the radio turned up to expel the anxiety of the interview from my mind, I drove home in a thoughtful daze.

As the Infiniti cruised up the driveway, I

guided it to a smooth halt. I had barely reached the front door before Brian shoved it open, questions lining his face. Grandma Ivie appeared right behind him.

"What did they say?" she asked.

"They said a lot," I replied, a bit smug.

Brian's brows came together. "That's no answer. Give us something to put our minds at ease."

Chuckling, I told him, "Whoa, whoa, wait a minute. Mind if I get through the door first? And maybe sit down?"

They both stayed on my heels as I headed toward the kitchen to get something to drink and a bite to eat. Starving since I'd been too nervous for breakfast, all I wanted was to unwind for a moment before recapping my day at The Bureau. That sounded so good: The Bureau. I kicked off my heels and flexed my toes, relieved to be out of those shoes.

"I'm losing it here," Brian complained behind me.

"I've already lost it," Grandma Ivie said from behind him.

I couldn't help but chuckle at how enthusiastic they were. Treading barefoot on the hardwood floor, I made my way to the refrigerator to get the rye bread, butter, cheese, and pickles to make myself a sandwich.

To cut down the time, Brian asked, "Cranberry juice?"

"One hundred percent!" I winked.

Brian poured me a cold glass while I hopped on the barstool at the kitchen counter.

"In fact, I am not sure, how it went." I told them. "I did the best I could and left it to their judgment." And then, I recounted everything that I remembered. They both listened so intently to every word that I could have sworn they were watching me like a movie.

"Worry not," Grandma Ivie said. "You're getting this."

"Agent Dyer seems like an ass though," Brian remarked.

My grandmother scoffed. "We don't care. My baby's already in the Bureau."

A few days later, before Brian returned to the Navy base, he said to me, "Make sure you contact me as soon as you hear something, sis."

"Sure, I will. You'll be the second one to know... right after Grandma," I teased, giving him a big hug.

About a week went by, and I found that I wanted to hear from the Bureau even more now than I initially thought. It became my routine to check my phone and voicemail multiple times a day to make sure I didn't miss that call from the FBI.

But I had missed nothing. There was just nothing to catch.

I kept myself busy with the boxing club, working out, and studying up on the FBI forensic training.

Brian called several times, his first words, "Hit me, Brea," to which I would reply, "You might pass out."

"Seriously?" he asked after three weeks.

"What?"

"They *must* have gotten back to you by now."

"Well, they haven't."

"Is that normal?" he asked.

I shrugged even though he couldn't see the gesture. "I guess so. Besides, it's the FBI. What can I do?"

"I suppose you just have to wait."

After I got off the phone, Grandma Ivie, who was sitting in her recliner chair, knitting, grumbled, "They sure know how to take their time and make you wait. Someone could be dead waiting on them."

I stared at her. "Grandma, some of the things that come out of your mouth are just hilarious. You, of all people, should have more patience. Didn't you tell me not to worry, to just keep the faith?"

"I did. But this is awful. It's already been three weeks. Didn't that Mattie lady tell you it would be two weeks or so?"

"Two weeks to a month, but no news is good news, I hope." These inquisitions irked me at this point. I could calm myself, but not if Brian and Grandma Ivie kept me keyed up.

On Tuesday morning, a full six agonizing weeks after my interview, the phone rang. It was Mattie.

No way!

I picked up and said hello.

"This is Agent Dyer of the FBI. Am I speaking to Brea Hellington?"

"Yes," I squeaked like an old floorboard.

Mattie got straight to the point, an offer to join the forensics department. Her voice echoed in my head, and I blinked rapidly as the implication of her statement hit me. My throat tightened, but I immediately accepted the offer.

As she rounded out the call, I relished the thought of driving back to Quantico in three days to complete my paperwork and get my badge and security clearance. I was thrilled at the opportunity to work at a well-compensated job with excellent benefits, but to have a foothold on the very career I had always wanted. Life couldn't get any better.

When I turned around, Grandma Ivie waited a few feet away. "Any news?" When I broke out into tears and a wide grin, she squealed with joy.

***

That night, I decided I wasn't going to read anything. I needed time for myself with myself. My smile was permanently glued on my face since I heard from the Bureau. My thoughts straggled here and there. Momma, my childhood, college, graduation, and the future. The future! What's in the offing? A dream career, money, a relationship.

Grandma and Brian formed the essential core of my life. Unlike other girls, I wasn't much of a hopeless romantic for guys. Scared of dating, I didn't think I handled romance and relationships that well. So, I stayed out of it, even if that meant staying away from men to protect myself, I didn't mind.

I found fillers to replace relationships. Everything but men occupied my time. While in college I always obtained stellar grades. I was great in all the biology and chemistry classes, seemed I was a natural scientist. Forensics was my dream job, and I had spent my time working toward that goal. None of the guys at school ever appealed to me beyond a pretty face, so maybe I was gay. Then again, none of the gals made me hot to trot either.

Whatever the reason, I was that rare breed of girl who was still a virgin at twenty-three.

CHAPTER

# 5

HEADED OUT FOR my first day at work, I was as nervous as I'd ever been. While I touched up my hair in the mirror, Grandma Ivie popped up behind me.

I jerked back like she'd scared me. "Don't do that, Grandma!"

"Do what?"

"Creep up on me."

She smirked, satisfied as a cat that ate a canary. "Oh, yeah, you're a Federal agent now. You might karate chop me into a coma."

I turned around with a laugh. "Is this your way of saying you'll miss me?"

"Nah. I'll miss you. That's my way of saying it." She ran the back of her hand down my cheek like Momma had so long ago.

After a long hug that almost resulted in teary eyes for Grandma Ivie, I drove to work. I was dressed in a fitted white blouse and navy slacks finished off with a pair of preppy Oxford flats. My Bureau badge hung from a lanyard draped around my neck. My hairline tingled from how tightly I'd pulled my hair into a bun; it was a fresh look but the one that I believed most proper for my work.

When I arrived at the front desk, the security officials scanned my badge. For a brief second, I panicked. What if my name wasn't listed in the database as an employee of the Bureau? My fears were soon allayed when an officer with a polite smile let me through.

After checking in, I followed the center aisle to the department where my office and the laboratory were located. The laboratory held the epitome of top-notch gadgetry among the well-placed machines. At once, I loved it. It had the feel of a dream. What more could I have asked for. I was over the moon.

Most of the men in the department stopped what they were doing to catch a glimpse of me from the corner of their eyes. A few stared openly as I walked, carrying myself with athletic grace.

The first few weeks at the job were hard. I was a rookie and goofed things up often. But the senior analyst, Mr. Henry Drake, made a patient mentor. I soon caught up and started handling things on my own.

However, I found myself yearning for a father figure who could share my experiences. Grandma Ivie was always ready to listen to me, but I still felt like I was missing something. The closest I had to a masculine figure, besides Brian and Daimhin, was Special Agent Boyett, my boss. I wondered why my father had left us the way he did at the funeral. A mild anger urged me to confront him.

Strangely, I had developed feelings for him. Deep down in my heart, I always liked him. He must have had adequate reasons to walk out on Brian and me. After all, we were his flesh and blood; the separation would have been difficult for him too.

*But if you want to meet someone, you must find them first.*

Fueled by my curiosity, I decided to quench the relentless questions that plagued me. While I made a place for myself at work, a plan grew in my mind. First, I would search the FBI database for my father's name. Then I would narrow down the hits until I found the right man. Meticulously I replayed every step over and over before placing the first wheel in motion. With the stringent rules of conduct, no evidence could remain of my unauthorized use of the database.

After weeks of thought, I walked to my computer calmly, as I always did, scanning the floor as I strolled to my seat. I opened the classified search tool. The software stuttered and then launched, as if it were winking at me.

In the name section, I typed *Daniel Hellington* and *Virginia*, then tapped the Enter key. I leaned back in my seat to wait for results, but the search was already over before my back even hit the chair. Forgetting my cool, I sprang forward to inspect the results. The screen showed eleven Daniel Hellington's, but considering age and race, only one fit.

*He doesn't even live far away!*

I memorized his work address as well as his residential address. Then, as calmly as I had performed the search, I cleared it from the local history. I wanted to clear it from the IT records, but such a breach would put my job in greater danger.

Now that I'd found my father, I wanted to know him before making any move. First, I should see what he looked like in person instead of pictures. I could wait to breathe the same air as him and touch the things he did, so long as I was learning more about him.

With that in mind, I drove to his office after work.

Prepared to meet the person I remembered from the funeral, a man with a hard frown and a tough façade, I waited for him to leave. The man who stepped out of the building sent me spiraling. His salt and pepper hair was black now. A smile plastered on his face, he walked out clutching his briefcase. No wonder Momma had fallen for his charms.

Flashes from the funeral fought their way up from my memory as I sat watching. He waved at someone as he made his way to his car.

For the next few days, I waited outside his office after work to get some idea of his routine. Before heading home to his family, he liked to stop at the corner bar on Florentine Boulevard for a drink. I sat outside, watching and waiting.

Once, he passed by my car as I stalked him. His fingers brushed my mirror, and as he walked past, I caught a slight whiff of his cologne. He did smell nice, like a mix of freshly washed laundry and citrus. How could he still smell that way after an entire day at work and an evening in the bar?

Determined to find out what happened between him and Momma, I needed a new plan.

CHAPTER

# 6

THE SOUNDS OF the Breakfast Show on the television filled the whole house. Grandma Ivie loved the show to bits, and she listened to it with the volume ceiling high.

"You'll go deaf with all that noise," I cautioned as I walked into the room. "And then what?"

"Well, I'd still have eyes to watch it." Of course, while she made breakfast in the kitchen, she listened to the show.

Once we'd finished eating and washing the dishes, I asked, "What's the point of TV if you don't see it?"

"There's a lot more to TV than visual stimulation."

I crossed my arms. "What else is there?"

"How could I explain that to someone of your generation?" Grandma Ivie teased. As I rolled my eyes and walked away, she snickered contentedly to herself.

"You win this round!" I admitted.

Seconds later, a breaking news announcement interrupted the broadcast. I walked to the living room to see what was so important. Grandma Ivie was already there, her hands planted firmly on her waist as if she intended to smack whoever was responsible. The news anchor handed over to a reporter who announced that there had been another murder.

"The county police released a statement this morning that the victim was male, twenty-four years of age. The victim was pronounced dead at the scene."

The visual shifted to a man in uniform with captain's bars on his shoulders. "This is the latest in a string of murders, and all evidence collected to date indicates a serial killer is moving from state to state. Local and state authorities have no leads on who may have committed these crimes. This is still an active investigation. There is no further information currently. Anyone with information about this incident is encouraged to contact the

Virginia County Sheriff's Department's Homicide Bureau."

"Oh no," Grandma Ivie muttered under her breath.

The reporter ended the alert with, "We will keep you updated."

"Things are getting out of hand," Grandma said with a sigh.

"Yeah," I concurred. "It's a brutal world out there."

"And you're out there a lot. Please be careful."

I smiled at her concern. "Aren't I always?"

"I don't know... This is just insane. Doesn't this make five?"

"I believe so." I slung an arm around her shoulder and guided her to the kitchen.

Grandma Ivie raised a hand, signaling me to be quiet. On the news, the anchor reeled out a list of the victims' names in the hopes that anyone would have information leading to an arrest.

"...Chris Hall, Toby Wyatt, and Steve Harper." the reporter concluded.

"One of those names sounds familiar," she said.

"For real? Which one?" I asked, even though I knew.

Grandma squinted as she tried to recall. "It's slipped my mind."

I smiled dismissively and gave her a peck on the cheek, thankful for the fact that her memory wasn't as sharp anymore. "You don't know any of those men, Grandma Ivie; you just think that you know everyone!"

"No, no, Brea, I have definitely heard at least one of those names before, I'm sure of it. I will think about it, and if I remember something, I will let you know."

"Sure, you do that. Look, the vics all are male—so far anyway—so don't worry about me. And I am always careful," I promised her.

For some reason, a part of me didn't want her to remember. I recognized two names on that list, both high school bullies. *Looks like they messed with the wrong person this time.*

# CHAPTER

# 7

ANOTHER KNOCK CAME at the door of my office, this morning had been busy. I had piles of paperwork and stacks of samples to process. The last thing I wanted was further disruption.

I glared at the door in exasperation. "Come in!"

The doorknob turned, opening to reveal an agent from the IT department hesitantly peering in. I knew him only in passing, but he always gave me his full attention. His eyes remained glued to me for as long as it took me to walk past him, but he had never said a word to me.

I glowered at him for a second and then got up to stand in front of my desk, resting both hands behind me on my desk and leaning back. "And you are?"

He slipped into the room and closed the door. "Sean. Sean Coby, and you are Brea Hellington, right?"

"That's what it says on the door. Is there something that I can help you with, Agent Coby?"

"Yes, there is. If you don't mind, I'd like to ask if you would like to accompany me to dinner this weekend?"

I stared at him, stunned by his brazenness. Since I had worked here, there had been the occasional passes made at me by the guys in the building, some ladies as well. I had made it expressly clear that I had no intention of having anything beyond a professional relationship with any of my colleagues.

Still that was no reason to be impolite. Except this was the third person to make a full-on pass at me. The first guy had walked up to me during one of the team's nights out to ask if I wanted to go home with him. The second lady had asked if I wanted a drink. And now, here was Sean.

"No!" I snapped.

"No? Why not?" He recoiled as if I'd bitten him.

I scoffed. "Aren't you married, Agent Coby?"

"What makes you think that?"

"I don't just think that. Don't insult my intelligence because I don't have time for games." I gave him a moment before demanding, "Well, aren't you? Just answer yes or no."

"Yes. Yes, I, I, I am. But. We aren't happy."

"I don't care whether you are happy or not, you are still married. Don't come to my office and disrespect me in that manner ever again. I don't date married men. In fact, I don't date anyone I work with." My brows dropped further. "Hold on, why did you think you could come in here and ask such a thing? Just who did you think I was?"

Agent Coby didn't answer; he simply averted his eyes and turned around without saying another word. He eased himself out of my office just as he had let himself in. I straightened up and took my seat. Still insulted I thought about Sean. Even if he had tried that song-and-dance number on every woman that came through the door, I didn't care. Eventually I managed to shrug my anger off, hoping that, for his sake, it was the first and last time he'd tried that line.

***

The smell of fresh pastries and rich coffee filled my nostrils. The scent wasn't real though; it was just my imagination working double time. But it was lunch time, and I needed something in my stomach. I also needed some solitude so I could clear my head and enjoy some downtime. I backed my chair away from the screen and stretched.

As I rounded the second-floor staircase and made my way downstairs, a male colleague walked up the stairs toward me. He made eye contact. Philip Decker, I realized, another agent from my floor and an acquaintance of Sean. I had only spoken to Philip in passing previously, nothing more than the usual cursory greeting. Today things were different; Philip stopped at the bottom of the stairs and waited.

When I reached the bottom step, I greeted him and continued in the direction of the cafeteria.

"Hey, can I join you for lunch?"

Although I heard his voice behind me, I thought nothing of it; he couldn't have been talking to me.

Philip repeated himself. "May I join you for lunch, Ms. Hellington?"

I stopped and turned on my heels. "Excuse me?"

"My name is Philip, and I asked if I can join you for lunch?"

"Why? We've never had lunch together before."

"I know, but I've meant to ask you to have lunch with me so that we could talk."

I began to size him up, wondering if he could have an ulterior motive. "So, Agent Philip, is all this at Sean's request?"

He gave me a blank stare. "Huh?"

I decided to play along. "Okay, sure, let's have lunch."

While we ate, I managed to get Philip to let his guard down by asking him some questions and reciting some witty anecdotes. At some point, I casually slipped in another question. "What's Sean's story? Isn't he married?"

"Yes," he replied. "Why?"

"He made a pass at me today."

"Oh..." His mouth twisted with chagrin for his friend, though I couldn't be certain of the genuineness of the gesture.

"Yeah. Sean absolutely did that."

"Was it weird?"

"Isn't he?"

Philip smiled just a little, and I could see in his eyes that he didn't want to put Sean down.

By the time lunch was over, I had decided that Philip was an intriguing guy. I still didn't do work relationships though. In any case, I was sure he was interested in me because I was a newbie, and the moment another female came on board, he, along with everyone else, would forget all about me.

I returned to work. So involved with my analytics, time got the better of me. When I glanced at my watch, it was quite late. I packed up for the evening. After I shut down the lab, I left the office and took the elevator downstairs.

Just as I spotted my car in the parking lot, Agent Coby's voice rang out behind me. "Wait up."

Instead I increased my pace, hurrying toward my car.

Undeterred by my clear disinterest, he sped up as well. He yelled again for me to wait up, that we needed to talk.

Irritated, I stopped and spun to face him. With my hands in my pockets, I scanned the surrounding area, checking for threats. I wasn't afraid of an altercation with Sean, but I needed to be certain he hadn't brought a posse.

When he was within a few steps, he scowled. "You questioned my friend Philip about me today?"

"Is that a problem?" I demanded.

"No. Just asking."

"Well, I did. Mainly to confirm your marital status."

"Why? He's not your friend, he's my friend, and that was out of line. Inappropriate."

Thinking how stupid that fool right there in front of me was, I took my hands out of my pockets, shifted my weight to the left and stood back on one foot. "Out of line?" I scoffed. "No, what's *out of line* is a married man asking another woman out on a date. Now listen, Sean, I don't know what you think is going on here, but I will not tolerate this crap from you. Don't ever again in your pathetic, meaningless life approach me with your bullshit."

"Well, Miss Brea Hellington, in fact, I came in peace," said Coby in a soft but firm voice. "I just asked you out. You could have politely rejected my proposal. We could have been friends at work or just colleagues, but your insecurity with the guys is way too much, I guess. There is no need to be bitter. I'm stepping back, and I am sorry if I offended you in any way."

I threw one hand out, like in a stop position, turned away without saying anything, and took the last few steps to my car. My heart thudded hard and rapid. Just before I drove away, the headlights caught Sean's hardened face.

# CHAPTER
# 8

THE KITCHEN WAS one of my favorite places in the house. The sight of its white cabinets and marble countertops always soothed me. One morning a few weeks later, I walked in and breathed in the fresh air coming through the wide windows. Everything was in place, everything except the one living thing that was usually moving around and making breakfast by that time.

"Grandma?"

I trudged to her room, the toes on my bare feet curling slightly as they contacted the cold wooden floor. I knocked lightly. If she wasn't awake, she needed the sleep, and I had no business waking her. Still, I was used to Grandma Ivie's routine, and I was a little thrown by her absence from the kitchen as well as the absence of the loud noise of the TV.

When I didn't get an answer, I turned the doorknob and peeped in to see Grandma Ivie still in her bed. "Grandma Ivie, are you all right?"

She was a light sleeper, but she neither reacted to her door opening nor my voice. Alarm bells rang in my head. I speed-walked over to her bed and sat just beside her. I placed my hand gingerly on her arm to shake her. Instead of warm flesh, the arm I touched was as cold as an ice pack. As though poked by an invisible cattle prod, I jumped back to a standing position. I hovered for what seemed an eternity, staring at Grandma Ivie's familiar face with alternating waves of shock, nausea, and disbelief. Seconds later, my training kicked in, and I felt her neck for a pulse. I closed my eyes and whispered an urgent prayer.

Nothing.

Grandma Ivie was dead.

Too weak to stand, I sat back down on the bed beside her. I stretched my arms to wrap them around her motionless body. The first whimper escaped my throat. With my head on her chest, I cried deep, guttural sobs for the loss of that woman whom I had known and loved my entire life.

*You've got to call it in.*

After I took a moment to calm down, I dialed 911.

The calm voice said, "911, what's your emergency?" but sounded distant, like a disjointed part of a receding dream.

While I waited for the paramedics, I tried to think, but my eyes continued to fill with tears, and my head remained empty. The longer I stared at Grandma Ivie's still body, the clearer it became— she was gone. Once the police and paramedics arrived, they examined Grandma Ivie briefly, but I knew it was just a matter of protocol.

No one could do anything that would change the cruel truth.

In a soft, sympathetic voice, the paramedic said. "Appears your grandmother suffered a heart attack in her sleep. Any health problems you are aware of?"

"No, she was always in good health. Just busy running more errands than usual. But nothing out of the ordinary."

"Anything new beyond running her errands? Any recent events that could have caused her to react differently or stress her?"

"Nothing that I'm aware of," I responded.

They rolled Grandma out on the stretcher. After loading her lifeless form into the mortuary van, they drove her away.

Suddenly, I felt terribly alone. Brian! I must call him.

I contacted the Navy at once to give Brian the news.

"Will he be able to make it?" I asked.

"We'll give him the news," came the reply.

At that point, I stood alone on the front lawn. The sun shone brightly, so wrong for such a somber day. A butterfly floated past. The sheer beauty was the most ironic thing, considering how horrible I felt.

How could you go?

When I was tired of standing on the lawn, I went back into Grandma's bedroom and took in all its contents. She wasn't coming back. Not ever. I tried to remember her smiling, but somehow, I couldn't.

However, I recalled one thing—as we sat together one evening, she said, "Brea, if anything ever happens to me, look in my bedside drawer." At the time I told her I didn't like such topics. Now here I was in her room, and there she was on her way to the morgue. I opened the nightstand drawer and scanned the contents. Under an old photo album was a faded envelope labeled 'Brea.' I ripped the envelope, disinterested but also frightened of what I would find. With a flick of my wrist, I let the contents fall on the bed. There were just two items in it: a bill of sale and a key to a safe deposit box.

A brief look at the bill of sale told me what I needed to know—Grandma Ivie had left her house to Brian and me so we would always have a place to rest our heads, just as Momma had always wanted.

***

After calling to notify my boss, I dressed, grabbed my car keys, and headed straight to the bank where Grandma Ivie kept an account. Once there, I asked to meet with the manager. When he approached me in the waiting area, I explained Grandma Ivie's passing.

"She left this behind." I showed him the envelope holding the safe deposit key along with the bill of sale to her home.

He couldn't meet my gaze. "I'm really sorry for your loss." He took both items from me and examined them. I wasn't paying him much attention, but I noticed he had an emotionless face. While he was trying to be genuinely sympathetic, his concern didn't reach his eyes.

"Come with me to my office." Once inside he motioned for me to sit. "Not that I don't believe you, but everything you've told us has to be confirmed. It's protocol, hope you understand."

I rocked my head back and forth in disbelief.

He verified my information on Grandma Ivie and our driver's licenses. "Now that I know you are who you say you are"—he showed a stiff smile — "I can inform you that your grandmother left instructions to be executed in case of her death. To access these instructions, we need you to sign some handover documents."

I sighed. "Where are those documents?"

The manager wasted no time in revealing them. After I signed them, the manager made copies and then invited me to follow him through to a private waiting area where the safe deposit boxes were kept. Once he unlocked her drawer, he stooped closer. "I hope you find something good." Those words reeked of sarcasm and condescension, but I wasn't sure if that were true or if I was just in a bad mood.

After he left me alone with the safe deposit box, I opened it. Inside were multiple documents. Everything that Grandma Ivie had owned, she left for the two of us. Her safe deposit bonds totaled three hundred thousand each, for me and Brian. There was an envelope with my name in Grandma Ivies' familiar handwriting. It read 'For Brea's eyes only.'

After opening it, I read Grandma Ivies' wishes softly to myself, *"If you are reading this, Brea, just know that I am with your momma. I had to leave one daughter to see the other. Life's cruel. But live your life. Find someone to love. Settle down and have a family of your own. Live a happy life. I wish you all that your mother wanted in life but could never find.*

*"I remember the day you asked me who Nancy Bremen was, and I know you have a lot of questions about a lot of things. Specially your parents' married life. And now is the time you should get the answers to all the questions that keep pricking your mind. In this box is the Bible that belonged to Nancy Bremen. Well, not really a Bible. It's your mother's journal, which she wrote in all her life. Not regularly, mind you, but when she needed to most. All the good and bad experiences of her life are here in her journal.*

*"A month before her death, your momma gave her journal to me. I still don't know why she did that. Maybe she wanted me to read what she could never bring herself to tell me. I tried to read it, but then I just couldn't. It was in bad shape, pages coming out and cover torn in half. Nonetheless, I encased it in an old Bible cover and placed it in Nancy's stuff.*

*"I almost forgot it. And then one day, Brian snuck into the basement. I followed him and saw him reading the Bible from Nancy's stuff. Brea, honey, he was too young to read such things. And*

*too brokenhearted. Worried that the contents of the journal may have a negative impact on him, I removed the Bible and placed it in this box for you to read when you come of age.*

*"Now is the time. Read the journal as a holy book of how things should not be done. I want you to learn from your mother's experiences and never repeat the same mistakes. I am sure you are stronger and wiser than your mother ever was.*

*"It has been such a joy raising the two of you, watching you grow into such wonderful adults, and I pray you live the rest of your lives in absolute bliss. I love you, and I am so proud of you. Take care of yourself and Brian. Love Grandma."*

Startled at what I had just read, I looked at the bottom of the box, there lay the Bible of Nancy Bremen's life. I clasped it to my chest and slid to the floor. Tears of sadness and joy overwhelmed me. "I love you, Grandma Ivie, and I miss you so, so much."

# Nancy's Journal

***March 18, 2004 Anniversary of Daddy's Death***

*Even though Daddy died in a barn fire in 1997 I believe I was 11, but I remember it like yesterday. I was on the other side of the yard, feeding the chickens, when the most petrifying scream came from inside the barn. The scream sent a chill down my spine, and I rushed towards it. I froze in front of what was once our barn, now engulfed in bright orange fire.*

*I heard the scream again from inside the barn, and I just knew that was Daddy. When I spotted him running around in a daze, arms flailing all over the place, his entire body was on fire.*

*In pure horror, I stood there, trembling and motionless, planted like a tree in a gale. I didn't know what to do. Daddy was screaming in agony, an anguish that I couldn't possibly understand.*

*The fire had engulfed the whole barn. Momma was shouting herself hoarse for help, romping in and out of the house with buckets of water, trying to douse the fire. And all I did was muffled my ears to avoid Daddy's galled screams.*

*Then his screams stopped, and I knew it was all over. His pain and the stinging smoke left me teary in my shock as I took in the choking smell of barbecued meat and singed hair.*

*Even as sobs racked Momma's body, she tried to console me. But her arms were weak around my shoulders, her head heavy as it lay against mine. It was the most traumatic time for Momma and me; we both lost the love of our lives that day.*

*That pain never really went away. I loved my father dearly, and he loved me the same but even more. Since that day I have struggled to deal with the overwhelming wave of emotions and devastation his death brought.*

*I am alive without him, but in many ways, it seems I am not. As I write this, I cannot breathe, the image of the burning barn suffocates me. I must stop writing now as I lack the vigor to continue. All I know is that I can never forget Daddy.*

### May 5, 2008

*I'm so giddy writing this. Today, while in Mr. Cousins' Trigonometry class, we had a new student. His name is Daniel, Daniel Hellington. As crazy as it sounds, it was love at first sight. He took a seat across the room, and I could not take my eyes off him.*

*I know I'm a sucker for a handsome face, and I hear it's a terrible thing, but you need to see Daniel to understand; he is perfectly made! He's biracial, but it doesn't matter as long as he's nice, and he sure looks very nice!*

*I've always considered myself an EOD - equal opportunity dater. I give everyone a fair chance.*

*Mr. Cousins kept calling my name, and someone had to tap me since I was so busy staring at Daniel. I couldn't wait for class to end so I could be first to introduce myself, and well, I fulfilled my mission. Daniel walked me to my next class, and as I talked, he didn't take his eyes off me. I totally melted on the inside.*

*The way we talked today was unreal; it was as if we had known each other for eternity. This is like a dream come true!*

### *May 10*

*Not much to write about these days, apart from Daniel, of course, but I don't have the time; Daniel and I have too much to do. I've been so busy spending my time with him that Momma complained today. She says I haven't visited or called her in a while. So not true, I called her last week. Daniel and I have gone past dating and now consider ourselves a couple! Yay!!!*

### August 15

*Daniel and I have decided to quit college and get regular jobs. Is that crazy? I'm sure some people might think so, but college doesn't seem like the best option for us. We have been together for four months, and we already know we want to be together forever.*

*So today we went to the courthouse and did something completely crazy—we got married! To be honest, in the farthest corner of my mind, I wonder if I haven't made a mistake. But I'm in love, and that should count for something, right? I do like the idea of it though; I'm now officially Mrs. Daniel Hellington. I couldn't be happier.*

*Daniel and I moved into my parents' place out in the country today, and I absolutely love it out here. It's very peaceful. I am sure Daniel will love it just as much as I do.*

### September 3

*Life is beautiful out here. Daniel takes care of me, but at times, he is just off the hook. He says things I shouldn't let him say, abusive stuff. I think leaving college and getting married and moving out here might be a bit much for him. Everything happened at such a frantic pace. We need to sit down, sort things out between us. After all, we have to support each other, face our upcoming challenges together. I am sure I can calm him down, help him overcome whatever is bothering his mind. That's what good wives do. Ha-ha.*

### September 22

*I recently discovered something. Daniel is the total package on the surface, but beneath all of that is a whole other person that I don't know, don't even recognize. I'm pregnant and not sure if the timing is right. We're both excited about becoming parents, but I'm scared of what Daniel is becoming. He watches my every move, and I am self-conscious all the time.*

*We have arguments multiple times a day, and he won't even give me a second to gather my thoughts. Sometimes I'm afraid, for myself and the baby. Have I married a bad man?*

*I have seriously reconsidered my choices. As much as I hate to admit, marrying Daniel was a hasty mistake. I should have taken more time to get to know him. I try my best to do everything to please him, but I miserably fail.*

### January 2, 2010

*The feel of this pen in my fingers is strange but comforting. It's been hard to get time for myself as Daniel is always watching, hovering over me.*

*A lot has happened in the two years since my last entry. My fairy tale marriage to Daniel has turned abusive. The verbal threats became a slap here and there. My stupid ass, I thought that would be the end of it. But things only got worse. Now, punches to the face, kicks to the stomach, busted lips, and dark bruises are a regular part of my day.*

*I'm afraid to go home after work, not knowing what to expect from Daniel. I was afraid for Brea and Brian for a while, but he loves them and takes care of them like a good dad.*

*But does he love me? I doubt it, though he still claims he does.*

*I feel stuck here. Love can't be this ugly and sickening. I gave this man too much control over my life. Now that I think about it, I should have left in the beginning, but I was always afraid of triggering Daniel's temper. I just never know when the mean side of him will come out.*

*I've had enough.*

*I have to be smart and plan my next moves to stay a step ahead of his lying ass.*

*For my personal safety, I should leave. But isn't it the duty of a woman to hold down the home? And ironically, I still detect a hint of the charming Daniel. My heart still beats for him, but deep down, I know my children deserve to grow in a healthier environment. I don't want them to think that this is normal.*

*I called the police on Daniel a few weeks ago, but instead of helping, their visit only made him more abusive, more violent. I confided in the few girlfriends I have, but they bailed. They'd rather lose me as a friend than face Daniel, and honestly, I don't blame them for being so terrified of him.*

*I'm working on my escape plan. I hope I can come up with a better solution than running blindly. This is my home, I know, and I shouldn't have to leave here, but that is just the way it has to be. I intended to renovate the house so that the twins would always have somewhere to call home. I guess that was just another foolish fantasy.*

# CHAPTER

# 9

I STOPPED READING.

For a moment I stared into space, my heart pounding at the horror of what Momma's journal revealed. As I held it in my hands, my lips pulled into a tight snarl. A lump in my throat strangled me. A fresh wave of tears threatened to cascade down from just behind my eyelids.

After a few deep breaths, I asked myself, "That was my father? He's a monster, a predator on the loose. I'd cared for this man in my heart, justified his abandoning us with self-concocted reasons, and longed to rekindle our lost father-daughter relationship." My former opinion of him left me with pangs of guilt.

Already following Daniel, not much changed in my plan. Just my goal. Instead of finding my father, I found an evil man who destroyed Momma, and he had to pay.

At the bar I'd make myself familiar to him. I'd encourage him to become comfortable in my presence before making my move. For the next few days I lost myself in Momma's journal and plotted vengeance for the abuses she'd suffered. Once my ideas formed a cohesive plan, I let my fury simmer until I'd tied up all the loose ends.

With my thoughts occupied, I let my regular life balance of work and boxing training slip. I could not afford to let myself become so distracted that people would notice a change in my patterns.

On the Wednesday when I planned to approach Daniel, I hit the gym. I had missed several days, and it was imperative that I didn't miss any more. Also, I expected the workout would focus my mind for our encounter. The gym always helped when I needed to clear my head.

As I slowly wrapped the protective tape around my palm, I filled my lungs slowly and emptied them with an exploding puff. I could feel the air rushing in and out of my lungs as I picked up the jump rope for a little cardio. A thousand rapid skips later, I was ready. As I started to pound my frustrations into the heavy bag, I felt my body resist a little. I hadn't been to the gym in so long, my body had forgotten what it felt like.

"It's only... been... a few... weeks," I muttered to myself. A grunt escaped my throat as I said the last word.

Jab, cross, jab-jab.

"Just a... few weeks"

Jab-jab, cross.

The strain gradually seeped into my biceps.

"I was chasing a bastard."

Jab-cross-knee.

My father's face came to my mind's fore.

Jab-jab, hook, cross, jab-cross.

He hit my mother and God knows who else, a voice in my head said. He left me and Brian when we needed him. He does not deserve mercy.

My arms really ached, but I kept throwing punch after punch. Buckets of sweat poured over me as I let out explosive breaths amidst rhythmic grunts. I threw my jabs methodically and felt the impact on my knuckles as the bag resisted my fists. My shoulders and biceps strained as I hit harder; I breathed deeply to center my mind. I was tired, but the more I thought about my father, the more I pictured him as I hit the bag ever harder.

*Jab-jab-jab, jab-cross.*

By the time, my session was over, I remembered why I loved boxing: it let me vent. I would be in pain tomorrow, but at least I had been able to empty my mind properly.

"I see you didn't need me today," teased Jake, my trainer, in an amused voice from behind me.

I turned with a half-smile that felt too sharp. "Just needed to do a quick in and out. Didn't want to bother you."

"Of course. I'm sure work is crazy, but I'm glad you managed to pop in."

I zipped my bag and slung it over my shoulder. "Oh, yes, I can never stay away too long."

"In other words, you'll be back soon, I hope?"

"Very soon." I flashed a real smile this time.

After a quick shower I took my leave, body and mind at ease. Everyone knew that boxing and work were my life. If I wasn't doing one, I was doing the other. Coming to the gym was a clever idea; Jake wouldn't read any meaning into my short absence.

My next stop was dear ol' Dad's corner bar on Florentine. It took me a while to adjust to the dim lighting, my neck tingling with anticipation. I expected smoke in the air, but there was none, just a faint tinge of pine air freshener and the slightly stale smell that comes with leaving your windows closed too long.

From the corner of my eye, I watched the only other customer in the bar. Daniel sat four stools down.

The bartender approached me with a practiced smile. "What would you like, ma'am?"

"A Hennessey. Straight."

"Coming up."

I watched him fix my drink.

Daniel drummed his fingers on the polished surface of the bar. "That's a strong drink for a young lady."

I turned in the direction of his voice and saw his profile as he sat watching the TV. When I didn't say anything, he turned slowly, deliberately. His features so much like Brian's, I almost let out a gasp when I caught sight of his face. I managed to keep it inside by holding my breath until I had to will myself to breathe. He had quiet, intelligent eyes and straight lips that made him appear noble, the same expression women found so attractive in Brian.

This could have been Brian from the future.

*Of course, this is Daniel. My father. Brian's father.*

To avoid making the moment awkward, I spurred myself to speak. "After an intense workout, this is how I like to unwind."

"Work hard, play hard, huh?"

"Yeah. But work harder is more of my motto."

He nodded. "Smart move."

The bartender served my drink, and after I thanked him, I turned back to Daniel. "What's the best food place around here?"

Daniel considered my question briefly and then moved two seats in my direction. "It all depends on what you have a taste for."

"Doesn't matter. I'm a food junkie. I like to explore different foods."

"You're not from around here, are you?" he asked.

"Nope, from further up north. Just visiting a friend." I got up to leave. "Thanks for the information."

Lines spread across Daniel's face as he struggled to understand. "But you didn't touch your drink. Or get the name of the place."

"I know. I don't drink." I gave him a wink as I headed out the door. "And I'm sure I'll find a diner on my way home."

I stood outside the door for a second, turned slightly sideways so I could see him. He was clearly thinking about our little exchange. Looking at my glass of Hennessy, he shrugged as if to say, *Good brandy should never be wasted*, and lifted the glass, throwing the contents down his throat. He turned his attention back to the TV but not before taking another look at the door.

I crossed the street and walked toward home, shocked that I had just been in the presence of my biological father while he had no idea I was his daughter.

But I knew who he was.

Our encounter held no dramatic significance for him. I dropped no hint that he had just spoken to his own daughter. He assumed Brian and I were miles away....If he even thought of us at all.

My lips curled in a sad smile. In truth we didn't exist to him. If we did, he would have known who I was when he approached the woman who looked so much like Nancy. Instead he considered me just another woman, prospective prey for his appetites.

On the contrary, our encounter filled my mind, threatened to choke me. I tried to suck down a breath, but imaginary hands squeezed my throat, threatened to snap my neck. Angry tears welled up. I might have looked composed, but inside I shook, rattled to meet the man who had contributed to my existence. He had been at Momma's funeral, and even though I was so little, I couldn't forget how heatedly he and Grandma Ivie had argued.

He hadn't checked on us since then.

*I have another life, another family*, he had said, without thinking of Brian and me or the fact that we'd lost our only parent.

His face bubbled up to my mind again. So kind and genuine.

Daniel Hellington wore a thoughtful mask etched with multiple worry lines, as though he cared so very much. He looked stressed, like those people who genuinely worried about others so much that it took a toll on them. That was his lure, how he got close to his victims.

How many more battered women would I find if I pried?

I had to learn who else he had hurt. I couldn't do that by asking questions. No, no, no, that wouldn't work. People like him knew how to cover their tracks. They knew how to make the victims feel responsible. They knew how to ostracize, alienate, and estrange their targets from everyone who loved them.

Just as Daniel had done with Momma.

I needed to check him out, starting with his criminal record. Records didn't lie. This time I'd have to use someone else's username and passcode so the FBI couldn't link my search back to me.

I was going to make him pay if it was the last thing I did. Oh, he would meet up with this pretty bit of tail again. And he'd regret ever hurting Momma.

That brought up my only concern: what would Momma think?

# CHAPTER

# 10

## Dear Journal

***September 2011 – Daniel Hellington***

*Laying here wounded and bruised. These days, I keep wondering if the man I married will also be the man who takes my last breath. It's too much to bear.*

*I do my damned best to keep them away from all the violence, I don't want them to witness their father putting his hands on me. Two weeks ago, the twins were in their room asleep before Daniel came home. This seemed like as good a time as any to confront him.*

*When Daniel arrived, I told him that I was leaving him. I kept backing away from him, as I knew that news would piss him off. Soon my back hit the kitchen door.*

*Daniel got up slowly from the table. With his fists balled up, he walked in my direction.*

*I tried to move away, but I had nowhere left to go. My eyes met his and I pleaded silently. When he kept coming, I turned my head away, afraid of what was coming next.*

*The blow I was expecting didn't come.*

*Instead his fingers curled around my throat. His grip tightened as he spoke in a low harsh tone. He told me to look at him when he talked to me.*

*Like I wanted to look at that asshole, acting crazy, out of his mind. I didn't want to look at him. Didn't want to see him ever again.*

*But I was losing oxygen as he choked me tighter and harder.*

*He said if I want to leave, I'd never get out in one piece.*

*I had to play nice and forgiving so he would let go of me. I begged for mercy, told him that I was sorry for wanting to leave and that I could never leave the best thing in my life. When he let go of my throat, I backed away like I was good and beat down.*

*And then he bared his teeth in a monstrous grimace. He turned around, swung his arm, and punched me dead in the face.*

*My bones just caved. I dropped to the floor, dazed.*

*He kept hitting me, and I just lay there. Blow after blow landed on my face. When his crazy ass had had enough, he stood up and kicked me in my rib cage. He leaned over me and growled, "Try to leave me now."*

*I don't recall much after that. Must have passed out for a while. When I came to, there was a light in my face, a bright glare stinging my eyes and warming my skin.*

*I was in the hospital, strapped to a gurney. I was cold, my clothes were wet, and I kept wondering if I had fallen into a pool or something.*

*Then I realized it was blood. I was wet with blood. My blood.*

*The darn doctor and nurse kept asking me so many questions: How did this happen? Who did this?*

*I didn't want to answer; I only wanted to know if my children were safe.*

*I'm back home now at least. I can feel the pain coming on again, so I'll write more tomorrow.*

### September 23

*I haven't heard from or seen Daniel since that last beating. His mother called to see how I was doing. She told me Daniel had dropped the kids off at her house and left. Said she would bring them home when I'm able to take care of them.*

*I don't care if they stay with her. She sides with her son all the time, but they are her grandchildren, and she loves them just as much as I do. And I do need someone to look after them while I recover.*

*Daniel is gone, I guess. He can stay gone, just as long as he takes care of his responsibilities with the twins. They are just two years old, and they need a lot, but we aren't going to struggle. I still have my inheritance that Daddy left to me; thank God I never told Daniel about it.*

*I don't want anyone to know how abusive Daniel was. It's humiliating to realize I almost let that man kill me.*

### November 1

*Back on my feet fully and able to get around by myself, I went to a lawyer today and filed for a divorce. Mother never knew anything about what happened; I couldn't tell her. If Daddy had been here, I would have had no choice but to tell him. While it's not what I wanted, he would have done everything possible on God's Earth to destroy Daniel.*

### July 8, 2012 — Last Attempt

*This is going to be a long one, but I have to write it down before I do something I may regret.*

*As crazy as it might sound, I contacted Daniel. I got his phone number from his mother. I was hoping that he would want to get to know his children. I was also hoping to confront him about the syphilis.*

*Yeah, syphilis. The bastard infected me.*

*I decided to be nice to Daniel and ask him to meet for a drink. When I called, I told him we needed closure on our history so that we could both move on.*

*He agreed. He sounded somewhere between confused by my request and curious that I had contacted him.*

*I thought we'd meet in a neutral atmosphere to talk things over. I had so many unanswered questions about why he did what he did and why he left us, knowing we had nothing. Why hadn't he told me about the disease that he carried, and why he had still chosen to lay with me and burn me in such a manner that I could have died had I not been diagnosed soon enough?*

*I arrived at the bar a little early and chose a table. Not long afterward, Daniel appeared in the doorway. His eyes caught mine, and he had the nerve to have this big smile on his face, like we were cool and he hadn't done any wrong.*

*"Shameless bastard," I whispered to myself and waved him to come on over.*

*He sat down in the chair next to mine and asked if I wanted to order some drinks or a bite to eat.*

*Sure, I thought, why not make him pay for it all?*

*He started talking animatedly about his new life and his new family, avoiding the reason we were there. I let him continue as I listened intently. My heart started to ache because this man had absolutely no remorse. He didn't even seem to have any interest in our past or excuses for his cruelty.*

*When the drinks arrived at the table, he slugged his down without hesitation, and I watched as he ordered another. "Nance, I know I hurt you, and that's why I left. There was nothing else I could do for you or those kids."*

*"Those kids, Daniel? Is that what you call your children?" I got all up in his face with that one.*

*Just to piss me off he said, "They don't know me, Nance, and it's probably better this way."*

*"No, Daniel, it's better for you. Let's get that straight. You and I couldn't go on as we were, but you owed it to your kids to be there for them, no matter what happens in life. You aren't there for them when they need you, when they are sick, when they have school projects or baseball games.*

*"You aren't there to teach Brian how to be a man." I'm certain I scoffed at that thought. "But how could you when you don't know how to be a man yourself. You should have been there to play football with him, teach him to ride a bicycle, anything. Just to show you cared. But you just took the bitch way out and ran."*

*He made a horrible attempt at a remorseful face. Head in hands, he rubbed his temples. "What else is there to say? I wasn't there."*

*"Oh, I know that too well!"*

*I let him continue to dig a bigger bitch ditch for himself, and he did. He literally said he didn't intend to be there now, that he thought it was best to start over with his new family and new life. He told me to leave all that past ugliness in the rearview mirror.*

*At this point, I just didn't know what else to say. All I wanted was to reach across the table and slit his fucking throat with the dinner knife that lay in front of me. I was just floored and speechless at that man's heartless responses. We might as well have been talking about one of Brea's stuffed animals.*

*I knew I was grasping at straws, but I asked him if he missed his kids.*

*This son of a bitch shrugged his shoulders and offhandedly told me that the kids were a part of his past. He said I was doing just fine caring for them without him, said he couldn't subject his new family to this drama.*

*Tired of the issue, he got up and tossed some money down on the counter like I was some cheap whore.*

*I ran up behind him, grabbed his shirt trying to stop him. I had to be yelling at him. "Just like that, Daniel. Is that how easily you can forget about your firstborn children? Your own flesh and blood?"*

*When he finally turned around to give me an answer, his face was as stiff as marble, his eyes as still as glass. That motherfucker said dead in my eyes, "Yes, Nance, just like that."*

*A ton of bricks dropped on my head.*

*He tried to walk away, and I tried to hold him back, but he was much stronger, so he walked casually to his car.*

*I clung onto his shirt, screaming, at him, "You will live to regret this, Daniel! You will live to regret this!"*

*Once he was good and gone, I walked to my car. I sat there for a moment absorbing the conversation. All the while I asked myself if that had been real. Did he really say all those things to me? Is Daniel that heartless?*

*I have my answer now: yes, he is. Daniel is a poor excuse for a man, husband, and father. He has made his choice, but someday he will wish he had thought differently.*

Tears ran down my cheeks and fell onto Momma's journal. I wiped them away quickly in order not to ruin the pages. A tight knot formed in my chest. As I read, I squirmed and shuddered, imagining the sharp pain of every blow Daniel landed on her body. My father had really hurt her, and Momma had nobody to protect her.

She never deserved such abuse. No one did.

I wanted to talk to someone about it, but I couldn't even tell Brian. It would send him spiraling backward, and he had made so much progress. The last time Brian visited; he mentioned a fair that he wanted us to go to. He even went to play basketball with some guys in the area. Brian hated basketball because of Toby, but he went. I couldn't tell him what that asshole did to Momma, not after the violence Brian faced in high school.

Besides he had loved Momma too much; he didn't need to know what happened to her.

I closed the journal slowly, too numb to think.

Daniel had been a fucking jackass toward her. Momma was too nice not only to Daniel but, to all the jackals in her life. I was glad that Brian and I never knew Daniel, no telling how our lives would have ended up if he'd raised us after Momma passed away.

I had a few choice words for Daniel Hellington. No, he deserved something more than getting chewed out.

When I tried to uncross my legs, I couldn't. They had lost feeling due to the lack of circulation. After a couple of stretches to loosen up, I knew what I had to be done.

That man needed to pay for everything he'd done.

The next day, I went to the office looking for an unattended computer I could use to run my search on Daniel. It needed to belong to someone who couldn't be tied to me, someone who talked to me every once in a while but wasn't a friend. I spotted just one possibility: Special Agent Boyett, my boss. However, I didn't want to use his code for fear of getting him into trouble.

Just as I was about to lose hope, Boyett's door opened; he was leaving.

Even though I had told myself not to use his code, he was my only choice right now.

Worst-case if Boyett caught me, I would be reprimanded and lose my career. If I explained that I was looking for my estranged father, surely Boyett would let it go, though I'd be under greater scrutiny when Daniel paid his due. That decided, I snuck into Boyett's office and shut the door before anyone noticed.

I hoped in my heart that his computer wasn't locked, but Boyett was big on security. The chances that he would leave the desktop unlocked were slim as I shook his mouse.

Damn, his computer was locked.

This was taking too long. Growing nervous, I was ready to leave when I noticed the laptop on the shelf behind his chair. I grinned as I lifted the top: unlocked. Today was my lucky day.

I rummaged through his files for the FBI search software. Jackpot, Boyett was still logged in. I typed a search for 'Daniel Hellington' and my father's criminal record appeared. Just what I needed.

Except I couldn't print anything. I didn't want traces.

As I was skimming the results, Boyett called out, "Sure thing, pal." His shoes clicked across the floor toward his door.

I froze. My heart beat so violently against my chest that I feared it would expose me.

However, his shoes clicked down the hall again. He was walking away.

I spun back to the laptop. It held only one thing of interest to me: a domestic violence case a few years ago. Daniel's new wife had screamed for the officer to stop making things worse, to just leave already. The case was dropped. The woman claimed they had been fighting, that her broken ribs and bloodied face were her own fault.

That was all the proof I needed. I closed the software and set the laptop back on the table. Just as I reached the door, Boyett opened it.

"What's happening here, Hellington?"

"Just checking up on my boss to ask him if he'll join me for a burger."

"Why do I think there's more to this?" He scanned his office for anything amiss. He had a keen eye, and I only hoped that he didn't notice that his laptop screen hadn't powered down.

"Can't I just ask you to come eat a burger with me?" I replied, feigning anger. "I wanted to ask your advice, but I figured it out while you were away."

"You sure?" Boyett asked.

I knew he wouldn't forget this encounter.

* * *

Two days later, I returned to the bar. Daniel was there, of course, sipping his drink. I laughed at the jokes he told. Though decent at conversation, he thought more of himself than he really was.

From time to time, he would lightly place his hand on my exposed shoulder and rub gently.

Goosebumps of revulsion broke out on my skin whenever he did that, but I managed to keep smiling and keep my eyes locked on his.

*Hi, Pops*, I wanted to say, but it never felt quite right, even as a sarcastic comment. He was my biological father, but beyond that I had no connection to this man. Brian and I were toddlers when he took off. Momma never mentioned him, and whenever we asked about him, any smile on her face would disappear fast. Sometimes she'd gasp and then reach for something to occupy her hands.

I always wondered why she almost cried whenever we asked about a lost love from so long ago. Now that I had read her journal, her reaction made sense.

Now I was vamping the monster right to his pretty face.

With no recognition he asked, "Do you want to sit in a booth where it's more comfortable and private, so we can talk better?"

"Sure," I replied, despite seething inside.

While sat in the booth, bits of Daniel Hellington's personality slipped free. He crowded as close to me as possible, and while his hands rested lightly on the table, his eyes roamed my body with shameless, vulgar hunger.

After he had bragged as much as I could tolerate, I asked him, "Do you want to go somewhere and talk some more?"

He nodded quickly and, after paying for our drinks, took me by the hand to the parking lot. "So how do we go? My car?"

"Maybe we should leave your car here and take mine." I pointed to my nondescript gray rental. "You can always come back for yours."

Daniel agreed without question. Whatever car we took was clearly of little importance to him.

I drove to the nearest liquor store, where I bought a bottle of Hennessy, and then went on to The Excess, a motel up on Roxy Lane. That whole time, Daniel's hands caressed my thighs, and I kept saying, "Slow your roll. I ain't running," to stop him from going too far.

After checking in, we walked hands intertwined to the room matching the number on the tacky keyring that the disinterested young man behind the counter had given Daniel.

"Room 620." He pressed the key into my palm with a lewd smile. "That's a lucky number."

Even though I couldn't see how, I nodded. "You're right."

"Finally!" Daniel whooped as I opened the door and ushered him in.

"Oh, yes," I concurred. "Hope you're ready."

"Of course! But let me go to the bathroom real quick. I got a lot of Henny in me."

I clinked my nails on the Hennessy bottle in my hand. "There's more where that came from."

As Daniel hurried away, I took in the dingy room. Nothing unexpected.

I sat on the edge of the bed; my toes curled in irritation. From my purse, I pulled out a tiny bottle of clear, odorless liquid. With steady hands I dumped a quarter of the drug into the Hennessy bottle. Once I'd given the liquor a quick shake, I poured it into the two glasses sitting on the bedside dresser.

Daniel returned to the room and gawked in amusement. "What happened? You don't drink, remember?"

I looked down, pretending to be shy. "I don't but this is a special occasion. I'll be shitfaced off one drink."

He grinned at my response as I reached for a glass and handed it to him. He drank the brown liquid in a single gulp while I put my glass to my nostrils and inhaled the rich aroma.

"The Henny don't bite, you know."

I nodded. "I know. I'm only savoring it."

"Like them wine connoisseurs?" Daniel scoffed. "What do they know?"

I placed my glass on the nightstand and reached for his empty glass to pour him another. The drug would soon take effect. His first sip of the second glass and he finally began to stumble.

"Careful," I said.

"Never mind me, I'm great."

Seeing that he had lost his balance, I took the glass from him just as he fell onto the bed.

He lay back and took my hand in his. "Who are you, sweet thing?"

"Just a girl," I said.

"Where you from?" he slurred. His eyelids drooped.

I didn't reply. Taking the little bottle from my purse, I dangled it over his face. "Do you know what this is?"

Fear registered in his eyes as he struggled to keep them open.

"It's a simple drug," I continued. "Gamma-amino-butyric acid. And you know what it does? It shuts down your nervous system. Feels like sleep paralysis. Pretty clever, right?"

His hands strained to move, the veins popping out through his beautifully toned flesh. But he achieved no motion.

For insurance, I pulled out some rope and tied his hands and feet to the bedframe. I stood beside the bed and snarled straight down into his black soul. "Daniel Hellington, you are a terrible man. You lie, you cheat, you beat up women. You spread diseases. Even after all your despicable deeds, you have no remorse!"

I wanted to yell, wanted to let my angry words come quickly, as they did when I was mad, but I realized everything had to be done right. I needed his fuzzy brain to keep up.

So I kept my voice level and spoke slowly, each word clear and clipped. "Do you have any idea who I am?"

Bewildered, his eyes held many questions.

I would be glad to answer them all. First I tried to sit him up, but he was limp, useless dead weight. I tugged at his shirt, and the buttons popped off one by one to reveal a physique that was slightly impressive. I then unbuckled his belt, unzipped his jeans, and yanked them down around his ankles. As I pulled his boxers past his knees, I turned my head. But I was just being squeamish; I was still going to see his penis.

My mission demanded it.

I retrieved a tube of crazy glue from my purse. After I waved it in the air, I slowly dangled it in his line of sight. Daniel's eyes bulged as he recognized what I held. I took his shaft in my hand. His body jerked very slightly as I squeezed a dollop of glue onto the tip of his penis, into and over the opening.

I screwed the top back on the tube and slid it into my purse. Perched on the bed I smirked down at his motionless, fear-riddled body.

I leaned in closer and placed my lips as close to his ear as possible. "My name is Brea, Daniel. Brea Hellington. Sound familiar?" I pulled back so he could see my face. "Surely you remember Nancy, my Momma? Remember how you beat her, lied to her, cheated on her? Remember how, just before you walked out on her, you gave her syphilis and didn't even have the decency to tell her so she could get treated right away?" My voice sounded far more controlled than my heart, which beat like a jackhammer threatening to break right out of my body.

Daniel tried to speak through his slack lips.

I shook my head at his pathetic grunts. "Don't worry about it, Daniel, or should I say Daddy? But that would be one big joke, seeing how you never stuck around for Brian and me. Instead, you went out, got yourself a new victim, and made another family. Did you hope you could redeem yourself? Redeem your sordid past after abusing Momma and refusing to support us?

"Well, it doesn't work like that, Daddy dear. That is just not how life works. You must be held accountable for all your wrongdoings."

"But you were right about one thing. Now that I know what kind of man you are, it was for the best that you stayed away. Our family would have been far worse off with you there!"

Daniel, in his drugged state, blinked his eyes rapidly to focus. When I got up from the bed, he tried to tip his head to follow my motion.

"Concerned about what I might do to you?"

His heavy eyes fell closed, betraying him, but his level of consciousness didn't matter. I was ready to fulfill my mission.

From my purse on the dresser I retrieved a yellow bottle of lighter fluid and a box of matches. One glimpse of Daniel's limp penis clogged with glue and a sardonic grin stretched my face. Savoring the idea of punishing this bastard, I popped open the tiny nozzle and squeezed the liquid over him until the bottle ran empty. Then I opened the small box and selected a matchstick.

Before I could strike it, the air turned cold and my arms trembled. The curtains over the plate glass window rippled.

Between the billowing curtains stood Momma's silhouette. "Walk away, Brea; he's not worth it."

My sense of justice warred against her compassion. "He deserves to burn. Here first, then down in hell."

Momma remained calm but firm. "It's not your fight. Live your life and let the man go. I should have fought harder."

I closed my eyes and gritted my teeth. Even in the afterlife, Momma was still a softie, still defending this brute. When I blinked she had gone.

*Momma, forgive me, I can't just waltz away and let this asshole live.*

Glaring down at the man at my mercy, my thoughts jumbled and clashed. Daniel Hellington deserved nothing but a cruel death. However, Momma didn't want me to take his life. Daniel Hellington was also my father. I shouldn't even be looking at him with his pants off, let alone handling his penis. I shuddered with shame and revulsion.

Don't be silly, I said to myself. This man? Your father? He was never a father to you or Brian. He wasn't even a decent husband to Momma. If anything, he is the monster who ravaged our family.

Poised to strike the match, I leaned in closer to his penis with my arm outstretched. Through a clenched smile, I hissed, "Feeling a little helpless, Daddy dearest? Well, let me tell you something: Payback is a motherfucker, but revenge is sweet." I scraped the head along the patch of red sulfur.

Before I could drop the flaming match on Daniel, the flame blew out, startling me from my revelry.

*This is murder. The kind of crime that I fight against.*

Frightened by the magnitude of what I'd almost done. I jerked up straight and backed away, my skin tingling at how close I had come. I grabbed a towel from the bathroom and wiped down anything I might have touched. After picking up my purse and the drug-laced bottle of liquor, I cautiously opened the door of the hotel room. Peeping outside, I saw no movement, so I stepped out and crossed the parking lot to get back to my rental car.

"You goddamn sissy!" I swore, mad at myself.

As I drove away, brimming with anger, I promised I'd finish this mission later. My hands cramped around the wheel. Daniel was far from the only man who took advantage of Momma's sweet nature. Once he burned in hell, the rest would join him.

## CHAPTER

# 11

AFTER A ROUGH day I slept fitfully that night. The next morning, I felt worse than I looked. I stumbled out of bed, showered enough to pretend I was clean and got dressed. While having breakfast the TV played a catchy alert tone, and the news desk popped up on screen. The anchor matter-of-factly announced that the Excess Motel on Roxy Boulevard caught fire late last night, one fatality confirmed.

*What the hell?* I screamed inwardly. *Did I do that in my sleep?* Had I set that fire while fully awake, but my mind had simply blocked it. My stomach twisted in terror, and bile lurched up my throat.

The report continued and I listened carefully. The fire had started in one of the rooms. Authorities suspected arson. The unknown victim's remains were recovered and sent for DNA analysis in hopes of a match.

I pressed a hand to my churning stomach and pushed hard. I expected Daniel to wake up furious at being naked and bound. He would roll off the bed and call the front desk to send aid or simply wait for the cleaner to arrive. He wouldn't tell any of the staff the full story because he wouldn't want anyone to know, including his wife. Though he might go to the hospital to get the glue removed from his penis.

Simple.

Instead a charred body was found at the motel, and my gut told me the deceased was my father.

The motel owner spoke into the camera. "This is a real tragedy, and I have no idea how my family and I will survive this. One-third of my rooms 413 to 622, all gone."

I barely managed to contain my shock.

Grabbed my keys and headed to the office. No matter how I felt, I had to show up to work, calm and focused as always.

Otherwise it'd raise suspicion.

On my way to my office, everyone I passed stared. I acknowledged each coworker with a

"Good morning" and continued my walk of guilt. Finally safe, I shut the door firmly behind me. I checked my computer for messages and the telephone for missed calls.

Nothing.

I slid into my lab coat and took my seat. *Had I killed my own father?* I entered my personal login information into my computer. Questions consumed me. A knock came on my office door, but it only registered in the faintest reaches of my mind. When it happened again, louder and faster, it pulled me from my reverie.

By the time I turned around, my boss strode in.

"You okay, Brea?" he asked.

Brows drawn a bit too much I blinked at him in mock confusion. "I'm fine, thanks. What's up?"

"Got word from upstairs that the victim from last night's fire was a Daniel Hellington. Relation of yours?"

"That, that was my father's name." Just for effect, I shook myself a bit. "I didn't know him at all." I kept my tone soft. Nervous perspiration trickled down my back. I didn't need anyone investigating Daniel's death. "My brother and I are, err, were estranged from him, absolutely no communication. We never knew the man." I sat at my desk trying not to fidget.

"Oh, I wasn't aware you were estranged, but I am glad to hear you're okay." He really did sound like he was sorry.

"I am. I'm fine. Thanks for checking in on me. I appreciate your concern." I gave him my best pageant smile.

"Okay, I won't keep you." He shifted back into a work mindset. "Are you still working on the Dawson file?"

I nodded. "I am. Almost done with it."

"Okay, good. Do you want your door closed or open?"

"Just leave it open, please. Thank you."

Boyett paused in the door to add, "If you need to take time off to—"

"Nah. I'm good."

The door closed.

In work mode, I was determined to reach my personal daily goal. I reached for my computer and pulled up the Dawson file. After a glance, I pulled up all the files on last night's motel fire, quickly scanning the evidence that had been accumulated so far.

I couldn't do it.

Instead I re-accessed Daniel's profile and read up on his second family. Like any agent curious about a dead relative. Daniel's other wife, Stephanie, worked as a college professor. Together they had three children, all younger than Brian and me, as expected. After confirming that they were two boys and one girl, I exited the file, then swiveled my chair around to face the window and lose myself in my compulsive worries.

Another knock came at the door, making me realize that my boss had closed the door, anyway. I looked up with exasperation. "Come in!"

Sean Coby stepped through the door. "I am sorry for your loss," he said hesitatingly.

I remained quiet, wondering what brought him here.

"Well, Agent Boyett, sent me his laptop for forensic analysis."

Oh God, Coby was working in IT.

"I didn't find anything, already sent the clearance report to Boyett." A slight smile curved his lips. "I thought I should tell you in case you're worried."

Perplexed, I stared at him with no words, just speechless.

"I think I should go, a lot of work today." He turned and walked out. While closing the door peeped back. "I was wondering if we could have lunch together?" He added, "As colleagues."

"Yeah, sure." It was the least I could do in return.

# CHAPTER

# 12

***March 18, 2013***

*I got a new job, such a fantastic opportunity. So of course, I have to screw it all up.*

*My new manager, Axel Crum, is interested in me. And I guess he is kind of cute. He has a squared jaw but very metrosexual. Stupid name though. Rumor is he changed his name after arriving in the US from the Virgin Islands.*

*The first few times we saw each other, we didn't say a word. Then today, he stopped to talk to me. He asked all sorts of questions, including whether I was married or involved with anyone.*

*I already told my friend Shay that I really wasn't keen on sleeping where I earn my money. Dating on the job is too risky. I mean, what if it doesn't work out? What if it ends badly?*

### March 19

*Just got in from a first date with Axel. He proved to be very persuasive when he asked me out today at work, and I ended up saying yes.*

*Our date was a little awkward though. His phone kept ringing, but he wouldn't answer. Says we can date but we must be discrete. He obviously doesn't want to jeopardize our jobs.*

*I'll see how this discreetness works for us.*

### March 30

*Now, my newfound relationship with Axel is so discreet that we hardly speak. He's very aloof, rarely picks up his phone or calls me at work. I understand but it still hurts.*

*When we do spend time together, he gets extremely aggressive. He barks orders at me, expects me to meet him in different secluded areas with lemon wedges.*

*Yeah, freakin' lemon wedges. Whenever we meet, within seconds, he wants me to give him some head. I usually gag and feel as though I'm going to vomit. I sure as hell don't want him coming in my mouth, but that's where the lemon wedges come in. Once he ejaculates in my mouth, I take a lemon wedge and bite down on it so that the juice can counteract his cum.*

*It's nasty as hell!*

**May 16**

*Axel hasn't changed. We also have a new employee. A woman. A few days ago, I overheard Axel giving her directions to his place. I didn't say anything, but I befriended her to find out what was happening.*

*As I was heading home from work tonight, I saw a car that looked just like Axel's. I wasn't sure as I glanced around to catch a better glimpse. I could have sworn it was him, and my immediate thought was that he was going to the new girl's place.*

*When I called Axel, he said he was at home. First lie. I let it go because I didn't have concrete proof, but I will know for sure tomorrow.*

**April 17**

*Samantha, the new girl, was all giggles, on Cloud 9. At some point, she said, "Ol' Axel, he's something else."*

*The way she said his name and the way she looked when she said that, my woman's intuition kicked in. I asked if she meant our manager.*

*That Heffa smiled and said he came to her place last night and they hung out.*

*I know the truth. Axel Crum thinks he's such a big deal, but in the end, he's a one-minute man. And she was still giggling when I asked her if she slept with him on their first date.*

*This fat cow said, "Naw, girl, we've been hanging out now for about a month or so."*

*I was furious. Axel had always given me the impression that he had no time to do anything, that he's either working late or doing some other pathetic thing. He would never really call me unless he wanted me, and whenever this happened, he expected me to jump when he said so.*

*And I did! Like some foolish middle school girl. Heck, even they don't jump that quick. What is my problem? What is my freaking problem?*

*I wanted to confront him right away, couldn't wait until I got off work. Somehow I made it to the end of the day. I need to cool off before I lose my job over this.*

In the semi-chilly environment of my office, I pulled my lab coat around me. I sat in front of the computer, slightly hunched over with my neck as tense as a bridge about to collapse. It was lunch time and my stomach growled, but I was determined not to eat until I had gotten all the information I needed. It was the first free time I'd had in hours, and I wasn't about to blow it on something as inconsequential as food.

Determined to run each of Momma's men from the past through the confidential database, I needed to get it finished so that I could move on with my life. My plan to vindicate Momma started with Mr. Axel Crum first, then the others. I took my time because it was better to be overly cautious than overconfident.

From the computer screen, I found that Axel Crum was the operating officer of a Fortune 500 company on Wall Street. He'd climbed a little higher up the ladder since seducing Momma. Never married, he and his male lover shared an ostentatious high-rise condominium in one of the most upmarket suburbs of New York City, where they raised a miniature Yorkie named Fifi.

I examined his face over and over on the screen. Arrogant and overbearing, I couldn't tell what Momma had seen in Crum. To confront him involved a 6-hour drive that would surely stiffen my back and cramp my legs. As difficult as it was, I somehow had to make it happen.

For Momma.

As I scrolled down his page, I came across a curious line: "Deceased: Cause of death under investigation."

I stood up from my chair, my lips parted slightly, and heaved a sigh of relief. I wouldn't have to drive to New York, plus the scum Crum was dead.

Eventually I turned back to the screen. I ground my teeth and glowered at Crum's face. *How did you meet such a convenient death?*

*Well, every dog has its day.*

I closed Axel Crum's file and pulled up the next abuser.

# CHAPTER

# 13

**December 2 – Dal Serpe, A new attraction**

*As a kid, I never went to the pool whenever the others were going. I was too ashamed that I didn't know how to swim. I always promised myself I'd learn to swim someday.*

*I signed up for lessons today. Tomorrow is that day!*

**December 3**

*I'm not sure what was more exciting, the lesson or the instructor! Dal Serpe is so tall and muscular but he's slender. Abs for days. Smooth brown skin. Strong facial features.*

*Get this, dimples on both cheeks!*

*He has a smile to die for, the kind that makes you cream your panties.*

**December 20**

*Been taking lessons now for about two weeks, three days a week.*

*And I've been dating Dal since the second lesson. So, I'm now dating outside my race but why not. I mean, he's just a man, much like the rest of them. He is years younger than me but not a kid.*

*It isn't an issue for me, anyway.*

**December 23**

*I don't know what's up with Dal. There seems to be something off about him.*

*But I won't let that get in the way of Christmas. When the festivities are over, I can get back to worrying.*

**December 29**

*I'm not so proud of myself, but I've been spying on Dal.*

*He's a serial flirt in relationships with a few other women from class.*

### December 30

*I confronted Dal yesterday. He didn't deny it—not that I gave him the opportunity. Instead, he became angry and belligerent.*

*How sad.*

*I guess I had hoped we'd have a real relationship with time.*

### January 8, 2014

*Yesterday was my final swim lesson, so I met up with Dal at the hotel to break things off. Thankfully, I had never let Dal come to my home.*

*Before I could say it was over, he forced himself in me from behind. Anally. I tried to stop him, but he was too strong and heavy. I begged him to stop, but he just thrust deeper inside of me.*

*When he was done I lay down for a bit, my body sore, drenched in his slimy sweat.*

*My whole body hurts.*

*Dal keeps calling but I don't answer. I'm so afraid I might run into him somewhere.*

### January 29

*Last night I woke to a presence in my room. I assumed it was one of the twins.*

*Dal was standing over me. In my bedroom. In my own home!*

*I froze with fear. I didn't want to panic or wake the twins.*

*He stood motionless for a while, as if he wanted me to embrace how real he was. Then he placed his finger over his lips. He told me that nobody quitted on him, that I had best be at the hotel tomorrow as usual, or he would come back to take what was his.*

*I agreed, terrified that he wouldn't leave. Seconds later, he was gone.*

### January 30

*I didn't go to the hotel. Instead, I made sure that the house was extra-secure before going to bed.*

### February 3

*Dal didn't like my blatant defiance.*

*For the past two days, after I've put the twins to bed, he's broken into my home. He forces himself on me, anal both times. The act is so painful that I thought my body would break.*

*I don't like Dal so near my kids. I hate to say this, but I think Dal uses his position as a swimming instructor to gain the trust of little girls like Brea.*

### February 10

*I finally contacted the police to report the abuse and get a restraining order on Dal. Of course, it was my word against his, and this angered him more. I've been getting threatening phone calls but thankfully no visits.*

*If I had looked closer, I would have spotted Dal's wicked ways a long time ago. I finally realized men who look good on the outside may not be so good on the inside. Daddy, I am so ashamed of myself right now, and I know you would be too. I wish you were here to guide me.*

As I looked at a picture of Dal Serpe on my computer screen, I could understand why many considered him good looking as well as harmless. He had friendly eyes and a gentle smile. His white hair sat regally on his head. That slight tan on his moderately toned body surely got him stares from the young girls.

From the information I gathered on Dal Serpe, he never discouraged them.

Dolphin Dal wasn't an Olympic-level athlete, even though rumors said he would have loved to have been. When he was much younger, he had won multiple medals, but he was simply too old for the competitions now.

Dal's records showed that he had never been married, but he was in and out of relationships with women closer to his own age. Typical of his sort, Dal created a shiny façade, that of a respected coach. That chronic pedophile used his position as a swimming instructor to fondle many little girls. According to the incident reports, he'd had minor scrapes with the parents of one or two girls, but none of the girls were willing to make statements.

The son-of-a-bitch had gotten away with it all.

He was getting on in age now, around his mid-fifties, but judging by his online profile, he looked to be in surprisingly decent shape. The Navy SEALs hired him as an instructor. Dal was well received on the Navy base, by all appearances a well-respected man. Dal lived on the Navy base and spent the greater part of his time training some of the toughest men in the nation.

*Must be difficult for you*, I thought, glaring at his picture. *You like them young and female.*

*And defenseless.*

Good old FBI resources, I'd tracked down Dal, and now I intended to break him. I relished the thought that such a terrible person, someone who wrecked the lives of so many girls and their families, would finally meet justice.

All I needed was a watertight reason to be at the Navy base as well as a plausible reason to meet with Mr. Serpe. After discovering that the Navy hosted periodic boxing tournaments, I called about the events.

"I'm really sorry," the tiny female voice said. "The base's boxing tournaments are internal, limited to sailors, but you are more than welcome to visit and attend as an interested recruit. Would you like to set up an appointment?"

"Yes, please," I replied.

"Your name?"

"Alexis..." My mind scrambled. "Alexis Beemer."

"We will send you details of the invite soon." If she noted my hesitation, her voice didn't show it.

"Thank you." I hung up.

As Alexis Beemer, I would show up at the Navy base and find a way to speak with Dal Serpe. Even if I was too old for his liking, I would find another way to grab his attention.

Satisfied, I focused on tackling a couple more files that my boss wanted in the next few days. I was always ahead of my deadlines, and I was determined to keep the momentum going.

A few minutes into my work, I remembered I hadn't heard from Brian in months. I decided to give him a call. I was concerned about him. Since Grandma's death, he had become more withdrawn, using his career as an excuse to disappear for months on end. I missed him, and I had been trying to get him to move back home so we could be closer. However, he had refused every time.

Shaking my head at the sad situation, a thought made me freeze. Brian was in the Navy. I hated to misuse my brother, but if I could get him to come home, he could get me into the base. I'd get a little time to spend with him and sink my claws into Dal Serpe, a win-win all around.

It would be great to go to the boxing tournament with Brian. He would even have fun. I'd tried to teach him to box when we were younger, but he never had much interest. While my timid twin brother had grown into a strong man, I doubted that he wanted to compete in the tournament.

I crossed my fingers and prayed that he would at least watch it with me.

***

I gripped the door handle of my car, mad that I was going to the naval base alone. Brian had refused to answer my calls or reply to my messages. As I climbed into the car, someone called out my name. To my utmost surprise, Brian stood in the parking lot, grinning broadly and waving.

I got out of the car in a rush, almost tripping myself over.

Brian and I raced towards each other. I was so overwhelmed to see my twin that I grabbed him by the shoulders and hugged him tightly.

"Hi, Houdini," I teased, my head buzzing at the sight of him.

Brian chuckled. "It ain't like that, sis. I got your messages, and I was going to reply, but I was just busy with military stuff. Thought I'd surprise you."

"Well, it's a lovely surprise. I can't complain."

"Oh, yeah, why are you headed to the naval base, anyway?"

"I just want to check out the boxing tournaments." I clasped both his shoulders in a firm grip. "It's so good to see you. You look terrific."

"Thank you. I'm brightening your day up already, huh?"

I smacked him playfully in the arm. We walked back to my car, arms interlocked, just beaming at one another. "So many questions I want to ask you, Bri, but not now, maybe later. You are staying with me at Grandma Ivie's, right?"

"Yeah, I'm staying with you, Bree. But why do you keep calling it Grandma Ivie's like she's waiting on us in the kitchen?"

I smiled slowly, a tear finding its way to the spot just behind my eyeball. "Habit, I guess. I always feel as if she's still here with me." I sniffed and rubbed away the quickly forming tear.

The ride to the base stayed mostly quiet. I was trying not to break down, and Brian understood perfectly. As we parked by the security guard's booth, he asked, "Hey, Bree, you good?"

"Yes." I nodded.

Brian investigated my face, and I grinned at him. It was an authentic gesture, for the need to cry had passed. He nodded in relief and kissed both my cheeks. Coming from Brian, that was a rare gesture, and it made my day.

The guard searched our faces. "ID, please?"

I asked for Brian's ID, and after he gave it to me. I arranged it in my hand, making sure it covered mine, before handing both to the guard. While he confirmed them, I distracted Brian with questions. If he had a look at my fake credentials, he would bug me until I confessed. I could either lie to my twin or tell him about my plans for Dal Serpe. And since I'd rather do neither, I kept Brian distracted.

"You're good to go." The guard passed our IDs back.

In a deft move, I covered my ID before handing Brian his. "Can you point us in the direction of the boxing hall, please?" I asked.

The guard directed me to the right and lifted the gate boom. As I drove at the requisite 20 miles per hour across the base, cadets marched past the barracks, posture stiff as statues.

"There's too much order in here," I grumbled.

Brian snorted as if he found that cute. "There's order in the FBI too."

"Not like this." I pointed to the recruits. "We don't march."

"Y'all too heavy." He laughed outright at that.

"Whatever, man." I grunted. "Is this how it was for you? Does this bring back memories?"

"Yes, sure it does, but marching was such a long time ago. Who would have thought that I'd still be here? But I honestly enjoy what I'm doing, and I couldn't have chosen a better job."

"I hear you. Same here."

We parked in the lot nearest the arena and then got out to walk. I might have smiled at Brian, but my mind was boiling as I kept my eyes out for Dal Serpe.

I found a sign for the Divers Hall. "Go on ahead to the boxing hall, Bri," I said casually. "I'll be there in a few minutes. Just like to see what the diving hall is all about."

Brian hesitated for a moment but shrugged it off. "Okay." He resumed walking.

In the diver's hall, I had the feeling that I had accidentally crossed over into another dimension. A calm energy filled the open space. The Olympic-sized pool shimmered in the artificial lighting, giving off beautiful blue reflections. The divers leaped off the boards, their athletic bodies cutting through the water cleanly. Then they swam to the ladders, creating a gentle lapping noise.

The divers made small talk and encouraged each other. They were working hard but still seemed to be having fun. I briefly wondered why I had always disregarded swimming.

"Back to the board!" someone yelled.

I glanced around but couldn't find the owner of the voice.

Two cadets walked past me, and the taller one, a lady, told her male companion, "Once you get this right, you'll be off to conquer the ocean. Now let's talk to Mr. Serpe."

I didn't react; I just watched them in my peripheral vision. After a few seconds had passed, I turned my head as if passively scanning the pool. The cadets stood by a heavy man with an oxygen cup over his nose and a tank over his shoulder. Upon further scrutiny of the paunchy man, I realized that was Dal. He appeared to be in poor physical shape, nothing like the profile picture on file.

*Must have been a damn outdated photo.*

It struck me that I had no need to meet up with him. No, a quick death would be far too kind. His pale skin and bent back told me that he was suffering already. With his current quality of life, I could leave it to karma to take care of him instead.

I stopped a cadet diver as he headed for the door. "Excuse me, I'm Alexis Beemer. I heard about the legend of Mr. Serpe. I wanted to meet up with him to learn some diving, but now that I've seen him, I'm shocked. I don't want to make him remember the good old days. How does he still train with his disability and all?"

The cadet winced at my question. "He doesn't train anymore. Nowadays all he does is observe and assist the other instructors from time to time. Back in the day when he was training, he was the best though."

"I heard that. What happened to Mr. Serpe?" I asked, barely managing to stifle my curiosity.

"Story is, while diving in the ocean one day, he accidentally hit something in the water and punctured a lung. He's been on oxygen ever since."

"Thanks for sharing, and I'm sorry for holding you up."

"No problem, ma'am. You have a good day."

I felt sorry for Dal Serpe as I continued to stare at his frail figure, a shadow of his former self. In his mid-sixties, he looked like death warmed up. He had hurt Momma, but karma is a bitch. Dal had already had his comeuppance.

Grinning, I turned and headed out the door in search of Brian. We could leave now.

The boxing hall was crowded with military units, seeming less colorful than the divers. But the arena was filled with passionate people, and I liked that. I scoured the bleachers for my brother's familiar face. I finally caught a glimpse of him waving in my direction. He'd saved me a seat.

Climbing up the bleachers, easing past everyone, I must have said "excuse me" a thousand times before I reached Brian. "You ready to head out?" I asked him.

"I thought this was what you came here for. Now you're ready to leave?"

Not wanting him to raise his suspicions, I suppressed the urge to grimace. "No, I just thought you were ready to go; that's all. Want to watch a few more?"

Brian nodded and I took my seat. The next match turned out to be quite riveting. Three matches later, we decided to head home.

After I parked in the garage, Brian and I climbed out of the car.

"Still treating this ride like a baby, huh?" he asked with a teasing sneer.

"It *is* my baby," I retorted. "Where are your things?"

He poked the bag slung over his shoulder. "Right here."

"That's all you have. Just a book bag?"

"Yes, it's all I need." He put a hand on my elbow. "I'm only here for tonight, Bree."

"One night, Bri? That's all you can give me?" My chest crushed at that news. "I haven't seen you in months. Wait, it's probably closer to a year!"

"I'm here now, so let's make the most of it," Brian said simply.

Such an infuriating statement, I almost yelled at him, but to avoid a fight, I walked to the front door. Once inside I asked, "Want something to eat?"

He gave no immediate answer, so I turned to find Brian still standing in the doorway. "What's wrong, Bri?"

He sighed and ran his hand through his hair, the way he used to when he was frustrated. "Every time I come home, I see Momma and Grandma Ivie, and it just shuts me down. Everything I see or touch somehow reminds me of them. The chairs? Remember how Grandma dragged us to go shopping for those chairs? And how she made me sew covers for the seat cushions?"

A sad smile made its way to my face. "You only made three."

"It felt like a lot more since Grandma made me re-sew anything that came out crooked. And remember how Momma liked to just sit in the kitchen? Those Saturday morning breakfasts? I..." His voice cracked. "I miss them both. I hate coming back home. I don't like to think of either of them as gone."

I walked back to the doorway and placed my hand reassuringly on his muscled arm. "It's okay, Bri; I understand. Just come in. Sit down." When I managed to get him inside, I asked, "Sooo, what do you feel like eating?"

"Whatever you have in the fridge will be fine."

I took two beers out of the fridge, grabbed the bottle opener out of the drawer, and snapped the lids off. I handed one to Brian and said, "Here ya go, nice and cold."

He held the bottle lightly between his thumb and index finger, his attention fixed in front of him, as if he could see nothing.

To distract him without talking about his grief directly, I put my bottle to my lips and took in a few huge gulps. I sucked my teeth together, let out an, "Ahh, this is good," and continued to drink until the bottle was empty. I wiped my mouth with the back of my hands. "Must have been thirsty."

Brian still sat, quietly focused straight ahead.

"C'mon, Brian, snap out of it. Everything is all right. It's time to move on." I handed him a bag of crisps.

He took it but held it in the same disinterested way he had held the beer.

As I set out to make him a sandwich, I opened the fridge again. This time, I noticed the empty spaces—no lunch meat, no tomatoes, no lettuce, no cheese. I turned towards Brian. "There isn't much in the fridge. We'll have to go out to the store really quick."

He mustn't have heard me because what he said next had nothing to do with food. "For about a year after momma died, I was just in shock, you know. Felt nothing but numbness. Barely existing in this world, moving from one place to another, there but not there, just a body in a shell. Every moment felt surreal, like it wasn't actually happening to me."

Before he could continue, I took the beer bottle out of his hand and wrapped my arms around him. Pulling him in close to my chest, I held him tight and took a deep breath as tears fell from my eyes. "It's all right, Brian." I cupped his face gently. "I know it was hard for you, and it wasn't easy for me either. I'm sorry you had to go through that alone; I had no idea. I kept wondering why you were not there for me, not realizing you were going through hell yourself. But I'm here, and you can always talk to me. I love you, Brian. Thanks for opening up to me."

I leaned back and, peering into his eyes, asked softly, "Are you going to be okay?"

"I'll go. You don't have to come."

Confused, I asked, "What are you talking about? Where will you go?"

"To the store. I need to get a few things too. What do you need me to pick up?"

I dabbed my eyes and grabbed a paper towel to wipe my sniffling, running nose. Somehow, I managed to smile. "Surprise me. Take the car keys.

I'll make sure that your old room is ready for you when you get back."

After Brian left, I went upstairs and found him some towels and an extra blanket for the bed. I sat on the couch and began to read a book to avoid crying again. I got sucked into the book, and when I raised my head to look at the clock, forty minutes had passed.

*Where's Brian?*

It was just the corner store; he had no reason to still be out. I called his cell phone, and the blare of his ringtone filled my ears from a few feet away.

I shook my head and sighed. *What the fuck, Bri? What's keeping you?*

# CHAPTER

# 14

**April 5-** Goddamn Dal is out and Ottis is in woohoo!

*So excited! Started a new job last week!*

*I'm working in a warehouse, nothing fancy. I'm working in distribution, on my feet all day packing material and shipping it out. It's heavy from time to time, but I manage.*

*I need to get a better pair of shoes though. My damn feet ache so badly I can hardly stand.*

*Today, this guy approached me, Ottis Strut, a smaller man, bit on the thin side, but he had this great smile, piercing blue eyes, slim face, and a smooth skin tone with alluring lips. I didn't want to stare but couldn't help myself; he's such a handsome man. He introduced himself and told me he was second shift manager.*

*He's management, of course. Like that wasn't trouble last time.*

*I'm not sure if I should be this excited, but this could be the start of something amazing!*

### April 13

*For the past few days, Ottis and I have been working close. We make eye contact severely, and I already sense a connection between us. I like what I see, and I'm extremely interested in getting to know him better. When he looked at me today, he made my pussy throb with my heartbeat. He got me so worked up and turned on that I was unperturbed by the fact that he was white chocolate, not dark.*

*This is work, and I shouldn't be getting involved with this man. It goes against work policy, and I would lose my job if anyone found out.*

*So why take that risk? He would still have his job and I'd be out on the streets.*

*Still, it would be nice to have someone to call my own. Some good dick too would be a plus, and Ottis looks like he could lay some pipe.*

## April 15

*I don't know how it happened, but today, Ottis and I just happened to be on lunch break together sitting behind the warehouse, everyone else having taken an earlier break.*

*He commented on my late breaks. I told him it made the day go quicker. He asked me how long I worked there. I said a year. He acted surprised, said how terrible it was that he hadn't noticed someone as beautiful as me for all that time.*

*I couldn't help but blush. I hope this becomes something more!*

## May 2

*I thought Ottis could be good for me. But he's just as bad as the rest of them.*

*It started with Ottis and I having lunch in his office, just sitting and talking. He called later that day, asked me to meet him at the hotel across town.*

*My dumb ass, I thought he wanted to talk, but he only wanted a head job, and I felt so disgusted.*

*Ottis didn't care. He insisted.*

*I didn't want to, but as my manager he could fire me at will.*

*This has happened a few times now. Ottis is rough and always has to have his way. I can still feel the stiffness in my jaw and the pain in my scalp from all the hair pulling.*

*I've gagged multiple times while giving him head, so today I told him about the lemon wedges.*

*He bought me a lemon soda to get the job done.*

## May 6

*Today, at work, Ottis had visitors. Women visitors, one older and one noticeably young and pretty. The older woman, a co-worker from another building, escorted the younger woman to Ottis's office, so I was immediately curious.*

*I asked Hannah, the only other woman in my department, whether she knew who the younger woman was. She didn't.*

*They stayed in the office for quite a while. When I saw them leave, Ottis peeked out from his office for a bit, all smiles.*

*The older woman walked right up to Hannah and me, said she wanted to introduce him to her daughter. Turns out Strut had wanted to meet her barely legal daughter for quite a while now.*

*I smiled politely and exchanged the usual pleasantries until they walked away, but I was unable to hide my disgust when my eyes met his.*

*Ottis turned away casually, as if he hadn't seen me, and then withdrew into his office.*

*After work I tried to call him, but there was no answer. This has gone on for several days.*

*I have to find another job. This whole mess is simply too humiliating.*

**May 7**

*Ottis finally called me back today and asked if I wanted to meet up with him to talk.*

*I told him that I couldn't keep going out of my way to meet up with him. It took time and gas, and I didn't have either.*

*He was like, "Oh c'mon, you know I will take care of you," and told me to meet him at the gas station on the street corner in front of the hotel.*

*Feeling foolish because I had let him talk me into this again, I met him at the gas station. I saw him waiting, so I pulled up to the gas pump. He pulled up behind me. I popped the fuel lever, so he could just pump the gas, but he walked around my car and stopped at my door. I rolled down the window, and he held out his hand, asking for my debit card so he could fill up my car.*

*I sucked my teeth and shook my head because I should have known!*

*He tried to act like he didn't understand, asking what's my problem.*

*I told him, "You said you would get my gas."*

*His exact words were: "No, I said I would take care of you. I didn't say I would pay for your gas."*

*Oooh, lawd help me. I was so angry, more at myself for falling for his trick in the first place. I opened my car door, hitting him in the knee, and got out of the car to pump my own damn gas.*

*He had the nerve to ask if I was still coming to the hotel. I wanted to know what was up with that young woman, so l said yes like the gullible girl that I am, or rather the nice girl that I prefer to be.*

*How stupid of me!*

*I should have gotten back in my car and driven straight back home.*

*Once back at the hotel, he wanted me to perform oral sex on him again. When I started asking questions instead, he grabbed me by the back of my head and pushed me down to the floor on my knees in front of his erect penis. He told me to open my mouth, but I refused.*

*He forced himself in and thrusted hard and deep down my throat.*

*I choked and gagged. I couldn't pull away, as he still had my hair in a vice grip, forcing my face forward. My eyes watered so much.*

*I just wanted to bite down hard.*

*After he was done, he handed me a breath mint. I stood up, in shock and disbelief.*

*When I was about to walk away, he grabbed my arm and shoved me down on the bed, saying now he was going to give me what I've always wanted. He forced my panties off, and since I was holding on to them tight with both hands, I heard the material ripping.*

*This? I never wanted this. What made him think that, I don't know.*

*He stood over me, lifted my legs over his shoulders, and inserted himself. I was so dry that I cringed as he forced his way into me. He was staring dead in my eyes like a maniac, so I turned my head to the side. I didn't want to look at him.*

*When he finished, he told me that if I told anyone, he would fire me. Then he told me to stay in the room for ten minutes after he left, that he didn't want anyone to see us together.*

*I didn't wait no ten minutes. I left right after he did, crying, running to my car, his nasty stuff running down my legs.*

*How could I be so stupid?*

### *August 10*

*I think about the way Ottis defiled me every day. I hate myself for letting my body be abused that way.*

*At least I found another job with better shifts and better pay, and I don't think there'll be drama.*

*I've broken off all contact with Ottis, but somehow updates about him still find their way to me. I heard that he married the young woman.*

*I shouldn't but I hope Ottis suffers. I hope he is unhappy in his marriage and feels pain in every part of his body.*

*But I can only carry on working and taking care of my family because I know my children need me more than I need any man.*

*As a young woman and a single parent, I've always searched for love, a love as deep as the one I shared with my beloved Daddy. But it seems the harder I seek it, the more elusive it becomes.*

*Today, it suddenly dawned on me what Daddy had meant about not letting any man hurt or disrespect me. Daddy, I still need you so very much.*

Ottis Strut was retired, still married to the same woman Momma described in her journal. They had six children and several grandkids. They threw parties, often twice a week, blatantly showing off their money. They had a small mansion up in the hills. It had eight bedrooms, a theater, a large swimming pool, and an in-law cottage. Strut also had four cars, a yacht, and a private jet that he never hesitated to use.

Strut hadn't always been that rich. Three years ago, he had won big at the lottery, about two hundred and sixty-five million dollars, and ever since he had proved himself to be the ultimate show boater. After a minor domestic incident, a neighbor told to a police officer that Strut was a big man about town, that his wife had become too good for any of her old friends and the children were spoiled rotten now.

I guess none of their peers liked them.

The Struts had forgotten their earlier lives. They had forgotten the days when they were living in a two-bedroom apartment with one car between them, working hard to make ends meet.

And so, the life of a factory manager transforms, I mused.

As I looked through the FBI portal, my mind worked double time. What could I find on him?

How I could make him suffer? While he and his wife and kids grinned widely in their photographs, Momma never had the chance to be that happy for any lengthy period of her life.

I dredged up my most psychotic ideas: Stabbing him multiple times till he bled out. Using a belt to strangle him till he turned purple, getting a cleaver, and chopping his round body to bits.

Then I froze. Death lets Strut off way too easy.

It dawned on me that hitting him in his pockets, now that would really hurt!

I decided to transfer his money to an offshore account, which I would open in Grandma Ivies' name. If I moved small portions over a couple of months, I could drain him dry, leave him and his family nothing. And the happy-go-lucky Strut would not realize what happened; he had no accountant, nobody to keep track of his fortune. The way he was spending, he would go broke in the next couple of years, anyway.

If I made the transactions untraceable through the FBI portals, no one would ever know.

Problem was, how to do it?

At that exact moment, the answer barged into my office. "Care for coffee?" Sean asked.

"You are God sent," I said in excitement, and he went to grab the coffee, none the wiser to what I meant.

All the same, I had to confront Strut face to face. As I continued scrolling, a red alert flashed across the screen, "DECEASED."

*Hell no!*

I looked again to make sure I had the correct man. Yes, I did. And now, face to face wasn't going to happen. Ottis Strut had been found dead just days earlier, cause of death unknown with no leads pointing to anyone.

Another one was gone.

*Damn it! What's going on? Why are they dying before I can get to them?*

Some thread must tie them together, but for the life of me I couldn't imagine what. I leaned back on my right foot, one hand resting on my hip and the fingers of the other hand pressed against my temple.

It would still be nice to have Strut's money though. And I could get it if it wasn't tied up in his estate. Hurriedly, I packed up and sent a text to Boyett saying that I wasn't feeling too well. He told me to get some rest.

After ensuring that I wouldn't leave any traces on my laptop, I headed for Agent Sean Coby's IP address. Gaining access to his computer was a cake walk. One plus side to working with the agency was the sheer amount of resources I had at my disposal.

Coby had installed a Tor browser on the computer I hacked. Through my own Tor browser, I arranged to move the funds by moderate automatic deposits into an account I created in Belize. On Strut's banking records, it should look like regular bills and the occasional splurge purchase.

# CHAPTER

# 15



***January 22, 2015*** – A Blast from the past!

*Guess who I bumped into today? Percy Allen!*

*It was great running into him again after all these years.*

*He still looks as good as ever! I had such a crush on him in school. He was one of the popular guys, so he wasn't interested in some shy girl like me. He only dated the popular girls who put out.*

*But he was friendly towards me, and we became friends outside of school. We didn't see that much of each other during school hours since our classes weren't even on the same floors. Instead we hung out evenings at his house or mine, watching TV or sitting in the yard just talking.*

*Seeing Percy today, it seems I have a second chance with him. I am literally as giddy as I was back in high school. He is more mature now, says he wants to date me, and I said okay. We exchanged numbers, and I can't wait for him to call tomorrow like he said.*

### January 23

*Percy called today, and we met up by the old school bleachers. Our date started out wonderfully, but today I realized that sometimes going back to an old flame just isn't the same. I was a different person, looking for something different and unwilling to tolerate some of the things I had previously put up with, but Percy was mostly the same.*

*He tried to kiss me right off. I had to push him back and ask him to wait.*

*Why did I even meet up with him? My dating life after Daniel has been one unwise decision after another. Moving this fast would only land me in the same toxic situation again.*

*Percy remarked that I was still not putting out.*

*I'd forgotten all about that. When either one of us had had the opportunity to drive to school, we used to stop at this popular spot where all the kids spent time together. Most times, Percy wanted to make out. Of course, I was too shy to make out with him, and he would get upset. If he was driving that day, he'd leave me.*

*I didn't care; it didn't bother me. I wasn't planning to let the world see me act loose in public! Besides, I was too embarrassed to let anyone see me kissing.*

*Now we've had just reconnected, and I want to at least get to know each other first. When he asked me how long that would take, he looked so desperate and silly that I had to laugh. In fact, I left him sitting on the bleachers, one of his old moves.*

*He called my name, but I didn't look back.*

*The house phone has been ringing off the hook since I got back. It can only be Percy.*

*Maybe I should just stop seeing him.*

### January 25

*I gave in to Percy, told him we could try again. So, we are going out tonight to a burger joint. I can't stay long; I have to get back home since I have work in the morning. I called up my neighbor's daughter to babysit instead of driving the twins up to mom's place. I'm in a rush to be ready on time.*

### January 26

*Percy and I went out for the burgers, and the night went fine. We talked for a couple of hours, then I had to get back home. No drama, no sneaky shit. I think I want to continue to see him.*

### March 11

*Percy's been tripping, beginning to change like Daniel. He has become physically abusive towards me. He now puts his hands around my neck, grabs my hair, twists my arm. He forces me to have sex with him and speaks to me in a derogatory and disrespectful manner.*

*The other night at his place, he terrified me. I left as soon as I could and wish I'd never spoken to him again. I don't want to be around him anymore, don't like his behavior.*

*But again, I went back for more. That time he almost choked the life out of me. He strangled me until my eyes began to roll into the back of my head and my breath became shallow. I tried to get him to stop, but he wouldn't; he just kept squeezing, and his grip got tighter and tighter.*

*He wasn't even looking at me. He had his head turned to the side.*

*I managed to scratch him with my nails, digging deep enough that it had to hurt. When he saw what he was doing, something came over him, as if he was looking right through me. He released his hands from around my neck, shoved me away from him, and told me to go home.*

*I needed a couple of moments to catch my breath, gather my wits, and regain my strength. I got to my feet, grabbed my personal things, and ran out of his front door, toward my car.*

*I wanted to call the police, but I was too embarrassed.*

*I attract the worst kind of men all the time. How do I bring all of this on myself? When am I ever going to learn?*

*Will I ever have anything good to write about in my life?*

*I need my Daddy. I guess I could tell mom, but she would never understand.*

***

*Percy Allen, yes!*

I was ecstatic to find a live one.

Percy was no longer employed. He lived with his girlfriend in a one-bedroom apartment, and she worked to support them both. I almost spat in revulsion; Percy was still taking advantage of women. He was one of the terrible men that had hurt and abused Momma. She had been too easy-going and too nice for any of the men in her life, and they had milked her kindness till the last drop had escaped her body and left her looking like a mummy. Percy Allen was also a lazy, unappreciative bum; he deserved to be removed from society.

Over the weekend, I took a short drive to set up surveillance outside Percy's apartment. All I wanted was a quick peek at the guy to see what was going on in his life, but if I'd kept an eye on him, he wouldn't have ended up dead.

Percy looked nothing like Momma had described him, but then again that had been a long time ago. The man I was stalking was extremely thin with a sunken face, as though he'd had a difficult, joyless life. He sipped from a little bottle clutched in his palm like a wino, and his jerky movements and clenched jaw told me he was also a drug addict.

The next Saturday I parked outside the place Percy called home. Using audio surveillance equipment borrowed from work, I listened to what was going on inside the apartment. For most of the day, Percy was alone at home, and most of the sound produced in his apartment came from television reruns.

Early that evening, a tall female entered the apartment, and in anticipation, I adjusted in my seat. Their conversation didn't take long to kick off. Allen said, "You're here, great. Make yourself useful and take out the trash."

"That's the first thing you say when I walk in the door?" she asked. "Not even hello. This is my home and I'm not welcomed."

Percy huffed at her comment. "I let you get in and close the door, didn't I? If you weren't welcome, you would have never made it inside."

Eventually, she said, "I'm not taking out the trash."

"Knock off the backtalk and take out the trash."

"No way in hell am I going to the back of the building; it's dark out there."

"You think you're so smart, but that's all bullshit. You're just a lazy bitch! If you don't damn well take out the trash, I'mma throw you down them there stairs with the trash. Y'all the same anyway."

I closed my eyes and took a deep breath. Nobody deserved such treatment. I wondered if the lady knew that at all or if she just felt she had no other options.

The woman's reply came quickly after, her voice spiking in intensity and loudness. "I'm tired as hell! I've been working all day, and you haven't done shit. All you do is sit at home all day, drink, smoke, and lie around, instead of getting a job. You take out the trash!"

I grabbed my car door handle instinctively, mentally preparing to rush out. I expected him to yell or hit her, but neither of those things happened. Instead, Percy stomped around, and when I heard something being dragged, I knew he had picked up the trash.

The door flung open and Percy appeared, an unpleasant scowl plastered over his already unpleasant face. As he lifted the plastic bag and slung it over his shoulder. He shuffled behind the apartment building.

I slipped from my vehicle and quietly approached him. "Did you know Nancy Bremen?" I asked, clearly enunciating each word.

Startled, he dropped the trash bag and spun around, hands raised to fight. But just as quickly, he relaxed, clearly relieved to see that it was just a woman behind him.

"Yeah, I knew Nancy. Who's asking?"

"Her daughter."

Percy Allen picked up the trash bag and tossed it into the trash compactor. He stood with his thumbs hooked into his jean pockets. "What're you doing here? I was at your momma's funeral, and you were just a kid."

"Shut up!" I yelled. "You remember what you did to my mother? Do you remember how you made her perform sex acts she didn't like doing? Remember, Percy?"

"Oh sweetie, we were young. Nancy was all into it; she even asked for it."

"Is that what you thought, Percy? Didn't you notice her tears?" I got right close up in his face and told him through clenched teeth, "Well I am here to teach you a lesson. To do what my mother couldn't do because she was a nice girl."

Percy looked momentarily confused. With a smug leer across his vacant face he asked, "Here to do what, little darlin'?" One hand reached down to adjust himself.

The fact that he would even think along such lines completely shocked me. My chest tightened and my arms twitched.

I considered launching at him and squeezing his thin neck until it snapped.

Instead I lunged at him, landing a blow to his throat and then to his chest in quick succession, both as hard as I could. Percy Allen staggered backward clutching at his throat and his chest. Pain and confusion in his eyes, he toppled forward, falling towards the trash compactor. As he crumpled to the ground, I gave him one last swift kick to the head.

There he remained, motionless and unconscious.

Though I wanted him dead, again I couldn't do it. I couldn't find it in me to commit murder. The sheer weight of taking another person's life made me rethink my vengeance. I wasn't raised to be a murderer. Grandma Ivie would think less of me if I killed this man.

Turning on my heel, I returned to my car.

Percy Allen would die another day.

# CHAPTER
# 16

LATER THAT NIGHT while lying in bed, I found I couldn't sleep. I turned over and reached out to turn on my bedside lamp. I opened the nightstand drawer and pulled out Momma's journal.

> ***January 1, 2016— Dear journal, smitten by the love bug.***
>
> *Happy New Year And his name is Daimhin Moderze. A Different Vibe, I Pray.*
>
> *I am finally done with Ottis Strut. I can no longer be involved with such a man.*

*A friend of a friend dragged me to a New Year's gathering at some club. I'm usually not comfortable around crowds, especially people I don't know, but I decided to do something different and accepted the invitation. It was a good night—I laughed, danced, and met new friends.*

*One guy caught my eye. I asked my friend for his name. Daimhin Moderze. Very appealing man in his own way. Now he's not the handsomest man in the world, but he has a certain air about him, that "lil sumthin sumthin" as Maxwell would call it. Daimhin has the perfect complexion, a smooth dark olive with black eyebrows, dark eyes, and dark hair. He is of medium build, not overly athletic or muscular but exactly right and tight all over.*

*As much as I wanted to just take him all in, I took it really slow; there could be no more jumping in with both feet. We locked eyes, and I tried not to stare, but I sensed a different kind of vibe from this man. Neither of us seemed ready to take the first step to approach the other, so I think he's as shy as I am.*

*I kept hoping that he would come my way as the night wore on. I didn't want any of those other women sinking their claws into him. When I turned my attention somewhere else for a brief second, I turned back and he was gone.*

*I kinda panicked. Had he left already? Had he come with somebody?*

*On tiptoes I peered over the heads of the people in the room, hoping to get a glimpse of him. Maybe he had moved to another room or maybe he met up with his girlfriend or something.*

*Sighing, I turned and made my way in the other direction, toward the restrooms. I turned the doorknob and it yanked me forward. Scared the hell out of me. While I was trying to enter the restroom, the very same guy I had been searching for was exiting it.*

*I stumbled into him. Flustered, I barely managed to regain my composure. Then I looked up at that rare and fine specimen of a gentleman's face. He apologized and then asked my name. I told him Nancy. He extended his hand to introduce himself. He said I'm Daimhin, nice to meet you Nancy. I just kept staring at him.*

*He was so much taller than me that I had to tilt my head way back to see his eyes. We were like Lilly and Herman Munster, and this thought made me laugh.*

*He asked me what was so funny, so I told him. He said he'd been born in Germany, so he'd never heard of the show, let alone seen it.*

*It hit me then that I really needed to use the restroom. This sweet man asked if it would be okay to wait for me so we could continue our chat. Of course, I said, "Heck yeah, please do."*

*Don't think I've ever been in such a hurry to pee in all my life; I wanted to hurry and get back out there before someone else snatched him up. When I opened the restroom door, he was standing against the far wall of the hallway, waiting.*

*Hours later, we noticed that most of the other guests had already left. The party was over. Our hostess, Natalia, told us that we should stay as long as we liked. I can't believe we had just tuned everyone else out for the entire night!*

*Daimhin walked me to my car. We traded phone numbers and said goodbye - for now.*

*This man is just too good to be true. I really like him, but I'm waiting for the other shoe to drop. That way it will be less disappointing.*

***

When my cheeks started to hurt, I realized I was smiling. Momma had found a ray of sunshine in our Daimhin. I had always known he was someone special, and it thrilled me finally to read about something good in Momma's life.

Daimhin never married, had no kids of his own. He had remained in close contact with Grandma Ivie. He never disrupted our lives, but he was always there for us when we needed him.

Why didn't Momma marry him?

I had work in the morning, but to satisfy my curiosity, I continued reading.

***

### January 2

*Early this morning, while I was just drifting asleep, the phone woke me. I almost didn't answer, expecting some random wrong number.*

*"It's Daimhin, Daimhin from the New Year's party." He thought he had to remind me who he was!*

*I was sure he was younger than me, so I asked how old he was: 25, five years younger. Oh, I was hesitant, but after giving it a brief thought, I decided that was no problem.*

*Daimhin asked if we could hang out, provided I had no other plans. I told him I didn't have any plans, but I had two children at home who would need a babysitter. I wasn't testing him on purpose, but once I said it, I realized how much his answer would reveal about his intentions.*

*He said to bring them along!*

*It was too soon for that, but I appreciate the gesture.*

*After I dropped the twins off at Mom's, I met Daimhin at the city Park and Ride so we could go in one car. After dinner we went to see The Titanic.*

*Such a great night! By the end, I was flying too!*

*I never felt this way before, not ever! I feel so cherished after one date with Daimhin. He may be younger, but he is a decent guy who knows how to treat a woman with respect.*

*When the date was over, Daimhin towered over me, placed a wet kiss on my forehead, and thanked me for allowing him to spend time with me! Incredible!*

*Still anything that's too good to be true usually is.*

## January 4

*Haven't picked up the twins from Mom's yet. They love being at her house and she loves them being there. I think it's good for her. She is better with them than she was with me. This arrangement also gives me the opportunity to spend more time with Daimhin.*

*Every day for the past three days we've spent laughing and sharing stories. I even opened to him about Daddy and how he meant everything to me.*

*I feel like I jumped the gun when I mentioned Daniel. There's nothing like ruining a great beginning with old trouble. I asked him if I shared too much, and he didn't hesitate to say no. I hope he was being honest. I guess I'll soon find out.*

*Hiding my past could bite me in the ass but telling him everything could blow up in my face.*

### March 3

*Daimhin and I have now been dating a couple of months, and things are going so well I'm ready to introduce him to the twins. For once in my life I am happy, and they should meet the one who makes me feel this way.*

*I've been holding my breath with Daimhin, expecting some bomb to drop, but it never did.*

*I've never let any man meet the twins. I might have messed up my own life by being easy, but I've protected them from my mistakes. This beautiful new relationship with Daimhin is going exceptionally well, so it's only right that he meets Brea and Brian.*

### June 18

*Recently, Daimhin and I decided we wanted to be together every day and every night, so he gave up his place in the city to move in with us out here in the country. He loves the secluded lifestyle, so peaceful and serene.*

*We spoke about marriage and having a child of our own! I'm so thrilled!!!*

*Daimhin is a great provider for me and the twins. He helps with the home and the finances. Most of all, he loves all of us. He has an excellent job with the Navy.*

*I'm so pleased Mom didn't sell the house after Daddy died. It feels like a part of him is still around. Plus, the twins love the freedom and the space to run and make as much noise as they like. Our home is filled with love, like when Daddy was alive.*

*For me this is a different kind of love than any I have ever experienced before. I just pray that, if this is a dream, I never wake up. Who would have known that you could feel so loved and protected even without being physically touched?*

## July 29

*All I can talk about these days is my life with Daimhin and the kids and how wonderful it all is.*

*Daimhin and I plan to visit his hometown in Germany next summer: him, the kids, and me.*

*I am so in love, and at night when everyone has gone to bed, I give myself to him completely, and it is amazing. We drink each other in; we breathe each other in. Our hearts beat as one.*

*The four of us have a family night once a week where we see a movie together at the theater and later stop for ice cream at the Triple Scoop, our favorite ice cream parlor in town.*

*We now visit Mom in the suburbs every Sunday to attend church. She appreciates how much Daimhin loves me and the twins. Everyone in her congregation knows Daimhin because she brags about him every chance she gets!*

*Mom is here more than ever. She drives out to the country a lot these days. Of course, it has to do with Daimhin. She adores him, and she sees me in a way that she never has before. I am happy, and she is happy for me. I think in a way it makes her miss Daddy.*

### January 2, 2017

*Something with my health is off.*

*My hairdresser has always loved my thick hair. The last time I went, it was so thin she couldn't do anything with it. Even my eyebrows and eyelashes—in fact, all the hair on my body—is thinner.*

*Then I noticed other subtle changes. I have a red dot on the inside of both hands in the same place and tiny spots on the soles of both feet.*

*What scares me most is a large white bump down there, at my groin. My GYN took a biopsy of the lump and referred me to a dermatologist for a second opinion.*

*I didn't mention that I had already seen my GYN when I talked with Daimhin, but I asked him to go with me to the dermatologist. I need his support.*

*Without a moment's hesitation he agreed and assured me that he would be right by my side, as always.*

## January 3

*The dermatologist knew immediately.*

*Syphilis. Stage 3.*

*But I'd had no symptoms until now. I couldn't understand. How had I contracted this disease?*

*I broke down like a baby. While Daimhin tried to console me, all I could think was, "It's over, it's over!"*

*The doctor reassured me that the disease was treatable and that it wasn't my fault, but traces would always be there. She gave me two penicillin shots and sent me home.*

*Daimhin held me close. He kept saying that it's all right, that it isn't my fault, that he's here for me. All I could do was cry.*

*I'm so embarrassed and horrified.*

*The next stage of this disease would kill me. The doctor said that, because I was so active, my immune system had kept the disease at bay. As soon as my immune system was compromised, the symptoms began to show up.*

### *January 4*

*Daimhin has his test results. He did not contract the disease, thankfully.*

*The CDC came to visit today. When they asked for the names of previous sexual partners. I only mentioned one name, Daniel, my ex-husband, before they confirmed he'd been treated.*

*He'd been treated and never told me.*

*I'm so furious with this man! The CDC had instructed him to contact me.*

*This is the second time Daniel knowingly tried to kill me.*

### *March 10*

*I don't even want to write in my journal anymore. I'm too tired these days. The syphilis outbreak took too much out of me. My trust in men is gone. Hell, I don't care to have sex, don't care if I never have it again.*

*I know Daimhin is struggling with the syphilis issue, but he tries to remain loving towards me. Deep down he is afraid. He stays the loving and kind man that he has always been, keeps reassuring me of his love for me. He even tells me that the infection isn't my fault.*

*Maybe Daimhin is the same and I'm the one who changed.*

*I'm unable to wrap my head around it all.*

*I still have not spoken with Daniel about this. He surely knew that he had contracted this disease and yet he didn't reach out to me. At this point I want him dead.*

## March 30

*I'm still in a blue funk, and Daimhin tries to be the same loving guy, saying he isn't going anywhere so I may as well get over it and start loving him again.*

*Daimhin asked me to marry him. It wasn't the most romantic proposal in the world—we were riding in the car and the question just popped out—but a proposal, nonetheless. He had a ring and everything.*

*I'm sure he hoped this would make me happy again, make us happy again. But I simply couldn't. Daimhin is still young and wants children of his own someday, something I can no longer provide.*

*As much as I loved him and wanted this life with him, it wouldn't be right for me to accept. Besides, he's asking for all the wrong reasons.*

*He responded with kindness to the rejection, saying that everything will be okay, and he will ask again another day.*

***

I closed the pages of the journal to take a breather and gather my thoughts. It was so much to take in. Some part of me wished I had read everything in chronological order. But it didn't matter now. I took up where I had left off.

***

### *February 14—Valentine's Day*

*No celebration here. Just not in the mood at all. So, I'll talk to my journal. You have gotten so old and raggedy. Your lock is broken. I found a piece of Velcro to wrap around you to hold you together. I will just pack you away for now until happy days return. You have served me well, much more than I ever expected when Daddy gifted you to me.*

*I don't want to get married.*

*Every time Daimhin is preparing to ask about marriage again, I shut him down quickly. Our relationship has become so strained that I asked him to move out today, and we parted ways.*

*It was not easy; in fact, it was a cruel, vile, heartbreaking thing to ask from my only true love, the only man who loved me just as I am. It really cut deep, but it had to be done.*

*He is such a good man and a good friend and an amazing father to the twins, who adore him. The breakup is hard on all of us, but as time goes on, we will manage to pick up the pieces and move on.*

*We never made it to Germany, sadly. This disease wrecked me, but I am fortunate to still be working a part-time job and earning a good income.*

# CHAPTER

# 17

*I struggle to remember dates and times. Mom told me the year is 2018. Dear Journal, you've been my best friend for a long time, but, Something's Wrong, terribly wrong and I'm afraid. I'm not ready to leave my babies.*

*These letters for Brea and Brian my final entries. I don't have the strength to continue anymore.*

*To My Brea,*

*As a mother, I pray that you and Brian find your own way in life and live happily. I have developed a terminal illness, enduring constant pain, and won't live much longer. You are still far too young to* understand anything, and I don't think that I will ever get the chance to tell you what my Daddy once told me: Take your time finding a mate. Make sure he is good for you and to you, but most importantly, that he respects you in every way.

I want you and Brian to remain close, so that no matter what happens in life, you will always have each other. I must admit to myself that I have made mistakes by being a careless young woman, sleeping with every handsome face that I met, trusting every word that came out of their mouths. I fell for every Mr. Smooth Talker, so when I finally met the one Mr. Right, it was too late.

In the end, he made me so incredibly happy during the time we shared together. He loved me, and he loved and adored you both. His love was worth the heartache.

Brea, if you ever read this journal, don't do as I did. I'm not saying it will happen this way because, in life, there are no guarantees. Just be smart and wise. I love you and Brian so much. If I had more time to live my life, I would make changes in my actions and learn from my past.

You should read Romans 5:3-4. Your Grandma Ivie always quoted those verses to me, but I didn't listen. The trials of life teach you patience, which becomes experience, which creates hope. Try to keep your virginity and your virtue both intact. There may come *a time when you lose your virtue, but you can gain that back. Once you lose your virginity, it will be gone forever.*

*Know your worth and wait for that special someone. If he knows your worth, he will wait until you are ready. And if he waits, then he is a special man. Don't get caught up in the good looks of smooth talkers with nothing to back it up.*

*There's no rush. You can still have a fun, fulfilled life in a romantic relationship without sex. Get to know that inner side of someone while observing the outer. Never let anyone take you out of your element or crush your beliefs.*

*I wish I could be around long enough to help you grow and to teach you about life, so you could live differently than I did. You are the strong one, Brea, so take care of your brother. He will need you. I know you will be all right.*

*Grandma Ivie will be there for both of you. I hope that Daimhin will remain a father to you, but he is not compelled. Tell them each that I love them.*

*I love you, honey, with all my heart,*

*Momma*

***

As I tried to choke back the painful tears, I whispered silently, "I love you too, Momma, and I miss having you around."

***

*To My Brian,*

*I'm sure you'll grow into an amazing, handsome young man. I'm scared though. Scared that you'll let life control you. That you'll let your early experiences in life color your view of the world. From the time I've spent with you and your sister, I can see that you're more like me. We let our feelings take over and control us. We let the lemons that life gives us sour our opinion of the world.*

*I hope that you'll be strong despite whatever you go through, but I fear that you'll let people walk all over you like I did.*

*There will be rainy days, Brian, but I don't want you to let them ruin your life. There will be days when it feels like all that's pouring is buckets of trouble, a storm of problems and bullies and evil people. I want you to know that after the rain, comes the sun. There will be sunny days. So, make the best of those rainy days. Prepare your mind for them and do what you have to find your sunny days.*

*I want you to continue to be close to your sister. You and Brea need to stand together no matter what happens. I trust you'll take care of each other.*

*And one more thing, my beautiful boy, always be happy. Smile.*

*I love you with every fiber of my soul,*

*Momma*

***

Tears welled in my eyes as I read my mother's last words to us. I was more than glad that Grandma Ivie left me this journal. Momma had been through so much, yet we were her priority. I needed to get that letter to Brian. He deserved to read Momma's last words to him.

***

I picked up my phone and read the text again: *Dinner tonight?*

I shouldn't need to think about my reply to Daimhin, but there I sat, hesitating. It wasn't that I didn't want to meet him. More I was bothered about how things would look.

After Grandma Ivie died, Daimhin and I spent a lot more time together. It started with him checking up on me, and now my day felt incomplete if I didn't speak with him. Even though we didn't talk about our increasingly romantic feelings, Daimhin's guilt spoke for itself. He hesitated, as if he were betraying Momma, even though their relationship ended decades ago. His words became flustered, and he often reminded us both that I'm young enough to be his daughter.

But I knew that it was Daimhin, and Daimhin only who stirred those special feelings inside me. The feelings that I had not experienced with anyone before.

I saw what Momma appreciated in this man. Everyone who spoke to him, he treated with respect. Every need he encountered, he met as an opportunity to be gracious. He still looked as handsome as Momma had described in her journal, just more mature with a soft mingled gray goatee. In decent shape, he was as active as ever.

His invitation to the spring art exhibition across town had been perfectly innocent. That night he focused on my well-being. He tentatively took my hand to see if I was okay with it. When I leaned into him, he squeezed with more confidence. Otherwise he was careful not to let his touch linger.

And did he make me laugh? It was as though his sole purpose was to amuse me.

That night he called to ask if I enjoyed the

outing. And then he called again the next night to ask how my day went. The more we spoke on the phone, the more I saw him as my friend instead of Momma's.

I knew what my answer should be: To hell with what it looked like.

*Yes*, I texted back.

He was at my door by 7 pm and drove us to a new restaurant downtown. Dinner was a casual affair. When we were done with our meals and waiting for dessert, his smile held a familiar sadness I'd seen a few times over the years.

"What's the matter?" I asked.

He shifted closer to me. "I don't know if this is appropriate. But I've..." His voice caught. "I've tried really hard to push it away, but I can't anymore. And I totally understand if you hate me after this, but I'd rather take my chances." He took a steadying breath, deep and slow. "But first, you need to know your... your mother and I... we had a relationship."

"I know, Daimhin. I know what happened between you and Momma."

He stared at me for a while as if weighing how much he should say. "You know your Momma was a really special woman. She always made me laugh, and I could tell her anything, and... she was just wonderful, out of this world. And I fell for her, hard. When she died, a part of me was ripped out."

I nodded to show I understood. "We all felt that way. But I'm sure she wouldn't want us pining over her loss after so long."

Daimhin scoffed. "Yeah, she'd have said something to lift us of this sorry mood I've created." The sad smile returned to his face.

I smiled back and squeezed his hand. "Sure, sounds like momma."

"I'm torn by this. So torn. It feels wrong, like something that shouldn't be, but I haven't felt this good with anyone since Nancy." His face flushed and I willed him to breathe. "Brea, I don't know how you might take this, but I think I like you. Heck, who am I kidding? I've always loved you, but I think I've fallen in love with you. And I hope you don't hate me for that."

Just the thought broke my heart. "I could never hate you, Daimhin. You've always been there for me, for us, when we had no one else." I let my gaze get lost in his. "You know I almost said no to dinner today. Afraid of what people might think if I liked you a little too much." A tug in my heart made me add, "Because I do. I like you more than anyone I've ever known."

His head shot up and his eyes widened in surprise. "Brea, I'm talking about love as in I want to marry you. I'm not talking about just a fling here. I'm talking about the whole thing."

A sappy, tingly joy shot through me. "I don't know about marriage right now, Daimhin, but I do know that I like you. I enjoy your company, and I can't imagine my day without you in it."

"You'll give this a chance? Give us a chance?"

I nodded sheepishly. "Yes."

The next weeks were like nothing I had experienced with anyone before. He was polite, chivalrous, and honest. Patient, even when I didn't deserve such kindness. I loved that man with all my heart, and I knew I would never find another like him.

We enjoyed each other's company, and we had so much in common. We were both workaholics who had never married, had never had children. We were both into investigations. From all indications, we were a great match, and I tried not to second-guess myself.

I predicted one problem: getting my twin to approve of our relationship. I decided to track down Brian and have a conversation with him. That evening, I called him and asked him if he could come down to Grandma's house for the weekend.

"I've got to talk to you. It's really important." I paced the living room.

The pause at the other end of the phone

seemed like he was going to say no. "I'm tied up in a project right now. Can I let you know by tomorrow?"

"But tomorrow is Saturday... fine," I replied. "Are you all right, though? You sound distant."

"I'm good. Just busy. Talk to you soon." He ended the call.

***

I woke restless. I needed Brian's blessing to date Daimhin, but I didn't know if he would show up so we could talk face to face. About 10:30 pm a car pulled up to the front of the house. I ran outside, straight into Brian's arms, and hugged him tight.

"That's quite the welcome," he said as we settled into the sofa. He looked tired, like he was carrying the weight of the world on his shoulders.

"I just missed you is all." I replied.

"Right." His knowing smirk made me smack his shoulder. "By the way what did you want to talk to me about?"

"Oh, that can wait till tomorrow." He needed to eat something and take a shower first.

"Nah. Let's talk about it now. It must be important if we can't talk about it on the phone." That was my insistent little brother.

"All right." I took in a deep breath but forgot to

release it until my chest insisted. "I've been seeing someone lately. And I really, really, really like him. He... he wants to marry me, Brian." Unsure how to tell him, I paused to think. "Bri, I'm in love with Daimhin."

I expected my brother to shoot out of his chair or give me a dirty, surprised look, but he just sat there. "Brian, did you hear what I just said? Daimhin and I have been dating."

"That's why you wanted me home?" He snickered as if I'd missed something obvious. "Brea, sis, that's not breaking news. It was only a matter of time."

I stared at Brian surprised at his reaction and confused by his words. "You knew?"

"I kinda had an idea. You two have gotten closer since Grandma died. I'm glad he was there for you. Half the reason I wasn't so bothered about leaving you behind was that I knew he'd treat you well."

"But he's—"

"Older than you?" Brian interrupted. "Doesn't matter. As long as you're happy."

This discussion felt entirely too simple. "Are you sure? He dated Momma."

"Look, all those things don't matter. It's been years since he was with Momma. And he's an excellent person. If he makes you happy, I'm good.

Momma and Grandma Ivie would have approved." He leaned into me and put an arm around my neck. "I love you, Brea."

"Then why don't you come home? What are you running from?"

"Nothing. I have no reason to run anymore." He sighed and kissed the top of my head before he stood.

"Anymore?" I called after him as he headed up to his old room, but he didn't answer.

A bit later, just as I was about to call it a night, breaking news flashed up on the TV. Investigators had found DNA evidence a short distance from where another young man had been murdered last night.

Heart racing, I connected the dots.

*No... No... No... Can't be.*

Brian. I guess I'd always suspected the truth.

I jumped up from the sofa the instant I heard.

*Laptop, I need my laptop.*

I hurried out of the living room and shot up the stairs to my home office like a maniac. Whipping out my laptop, I logged into the database to search for images of the evidence that they had found.

I found a picture of an Eiffel Tower key chain holding a broken and bloody glass ampule. And even though it had been years since I last saw it, it had to be the same one I gave to Brian all those years ago.

I fell to the carpet in shock. This was just a coincidence, right? Except all the men that had treated Momma badly had wound up dead. Two of the boys who bullied Brian had wound up dead. And now, they found a bookmark I suspected was mine. The last murder had happened while Brian was busy last night. What were the odds?

I had to convince Brian to stop.

*Momma's journal.* Is that why he shut everyone out?

I thought of the letter Momma had written. Stand together no matter what, she'd said. He couldn't have read the whole thing.

Percy Allen was still wheezing after all.

I sent the image of the key chain to my printer and tore Momma's letter for Brian from her journal. Momma had asked him not to let his experiences ruin his future. Maybe if he wouldn't listen to me, he'd listen to Momma.

The printer spurted out the image of the key chain. I cut it out, then wrapped the small image in the letter Momma wrote. I headed for Brian's room. I knocked on the door and pushed it open.

Brian stood, staring at me in surprise.

I walked up to him and handed him the bundle. "I've got your back, little brother."

"Don't call me that!" he replied without heat.

I said nothing more. Hopefully he understood my message.

He said earlier that he wasn't running anymore. If he had finished what he started, he'd come home more. Maybe.

CHAPTER

# 18

STANDING BEFORE THE mirror a rush of emotions overpowered me. At that moment, I must have been the prettiest thing in the world. I looked gorgeous in the wedding dress I had chosen, if I did say so myself. My hair was in an updo with a few spiral curls draped softly around my face. I twirled in front of the mirror like some fairytale princess.

I felt the tears coming and took deep breaths to dismiss them. If only Momma and Grandma Ivie were in attendance, today would have been perfect. I wanted so much for Momma to walk me down the aisle, but I had the next best thing, Brian. He had flown in for the wedding.

Standing arm-in-arm with my brother, I felt on top of the world. "I wish Momma and Grandma were here."

"Me too," Brian whispered back. "But I'm sure they wouldn't want you sad on your wedding day." He planted a kiss on my temple. "You look amazing."

"Thanks, Bri. And thanks for coming."

"Don't thank me. I would never miss this for anything in the world. There is no way I could let you get married without your better half in attendance."

I wanted to laugh but the butterflies in my stomach wouldn't let me. "Are you sure, though? About Daimhin?"

"I have no issues with this, Brea. I can't think of anyone more worthy of you. Daimhin and I never lost contact, so I kind of already knew before you started dating. He wanted my blessing and I gave it to him."

I would have stopped the ceremony itself to gape at him over that news. "Wait, what?"

"Yeah. Daimhin confided in me first to see how I felt before getting involved with you. Let's just say we both concluded that Momma would approve."

"Oh, Brian." Tears welled up behind my eyes.

"Enough reminiscing. Let's get you married."

The wedding was relatively small, a dozen guests in attendance, if that. I never had time for girlfriends, so there were no bridesmaids or matron of honor. Only Momma and Grandma had been that close to me.

When the doors opened, I gasped in surprise. As small as the wedding was, I loved the look. The deep reds and oranges of the decor reminded me of a fall day, and the white roses stacked around the church filled my nostrils with a sweet aroma.

Arm locked with Brian's; I scanned the front of the room for the love of my life. He was standing at the end of the main aisle, more handsome than ever. My eyes locked on Daimhin, and his on me. No one else mattered. When the music started, I took my first step. The tears at the back of my eyes started to sting, threatening to fall and ruin my makeup.

Our love palpable, it filled the church.

Brian walked me down the aisle. "I'm so proud of you. And Momma would be too." The thought made me grin as wide as he did. "This would be one of Momma's sunny days, the end to all those rainy days."

Breaking my gaze from Daimhin, I peered up at Brian, surprised. *Those rainy days.* He'd read the rest of Momma's journal, but how? When?

He smiled at me with a twinkle in his eyes.

There was no way I could react, not at that moment. I held onto my twin's arm, trying not to look up at him. Nothing would disrupt the best day of my life. I focused on my future husband waiting for me in front of the altar while Brian and I walked slowly down the aisle.

*Those rainy days.* I blinked rapidly and hoped no one could see the confusion ripping through me.

When we arrived at the altar, Brian held onto my hand as he told Daimhin, "I know you'll take loving care of my sister. Protect her. From herself."

Daimhin nodded and both men shook hands. Turning towards me, Brian planted a kiss on my forehead and stood beside Daimhin as his best man. I just smiled at my baby brother and turned to face the pastor who started with a prayer.

During the vows, Brian handed the pastor the wedding bands. Daimhin had bought me the most exquisite yellow diamond ring I had ever seen. Breathtaking. I couldn't stop staring. The ring was just as perfect as the day.

Once all the *I dos* were done and the rings exchanged, we kissed. I wanted to stop for decency's sake, but I couldn't. The cheers and laughter from our guests finally broke us apart.

"Ladies and gentlemen," the pastor called in excitement, "I present to you, Mr. and Mrs. Daimhin Moderze!"

My heart almost burst in my ribcage. This time, I couldn't help the flood of tears that streamed down my face. Daimhin, my husband, pulled me into his arms.

For that moment, I felt safe.

We turned to face the small crowd and received applause so loud that I wondered where the two hundred extra guests were hiding. We held hands as we floated down the aisle to the door, smiling all the way.

We strutted into the wedding reception amidst cheers and confetti. While we danced I couldn't wait to be alone with my husband.

My husband. The best words ever spoken; I was filled with joy.

After the throwing of the bouquet, we headed straight to the airport to catch a direct flight to Paris for our two-week honeymoon.

All the while, my heart thudded. I struggled to process Brian's words. Why couldn't we have been the kind of twins that could read each other's minds?

***

During the taxi ride the lights of Paris left my eyes tingling. As Daimhin's warm palm slipped into mine, I bit my lip, joyful to have him. We pulled to a stop at the romantic Le Bristol Paris hotel, where we would pay two thousand dollars per night for the privilege.

When he mentioned the cost, I almost fell over. "Isn't that a little too much?"

"Nah, no such thing. We only get one honeymoon, and I know the experience is worth every penny."

The sight from our window was every bit as beautiful as the guidebook had described. The skyline shimmered on the horizon, dotted by trees and gently curved hills. I was so excited; I had always wanted to visit Paris, and I could hardly believe I was here. I was in Paris and in love, and things were going great. I had to pinch myself to be sure it was all real.

Even so I blushed with guilt at the things I had done: stalking those men, punishing my father, stealing money from a dead man. But Momma's suffering needed to be addressed, and those wicked men had all gotten what they deserved. Or that was how I justified it. I wasn't going to bother myself with that anymore.

I was going to be happy.

"Daimhin!" I called out to him, "I know, when you were with Momma, you said one day you would take us all to your hometown in Germany."

"Let's not talk about that now, Bree, please."

"Okay, I understand, not the right time."

He kissed me on the forehead. Then, we stood and watched the sunset, the view more amazing than any I had ever seen before.

"Would you like a glass of wine?" he asked.

"Yes, please. You pour; I'm going to change for the evening. I'll be right back." I kissed him on the cheek and went into the bathroom where I had a cute lace negligee laid out.

Nerves bit at me. At 30 I'd never been with a man, not in that way. Momma and Grandma Ivie would have been so proud that I'd kept myself.

Now, if only we could get Brian married... or even dating! Then I thought back to what Brian had said as he walked me down the aisle.

I had a tough time accepting that he had been responsible for some of Momma's past lovers' deaths. How was my sweet-tempered, gentle-nature brother capable of such a thing? It had seemed so odd that some of those men had turned up dead before I got the chance to speak with them, while others I had left to live their misery-filled lives had ended up dead.

I recalled all the serial killings of the young men in their late twenties, how some turned out to be the same guys who bullied Brian in high school. *My little brother was responsible for those murders too?*

And what about our father? He'd been alive when I'd left.

I didn't want to question Brian, so I resolved to leave it alone. We were both in a much better place. I had tainted the evidence against Brian with bacterial DNA, so there was no reason to think on it any further.

***

New beginnings are also endings. Though my life in our family home had ended, I kept Grandma Ivies' house for Brian, for when he decided to retire from the Navy, and why not? Momma and Grandma Ivie would have wanted no other way.

Daimhin and I shared his beautiful home in the city, close to both our jobs. At forty-five hundred square feet, his loft condominium was as luxurious as it was discreet. Designed with sunken marble floors and an extravagant view of the city, I adored it.

I didn't have much to move in. All the furniture back at home was Grandma Ivie's, so I packed my clothes into the Infiniti.

"Why in the world do you still have this car?" Daimhin asked as he put one of the boxes in the boot.

"Because I love it?" I offered.

"It's time you got a new car, Brea."

"Nope. I love this one. Now stop talking so much and help move these boxes."

Later, as I unpacked my things, I noticed a large envelope in the mail from Grandma Ivie's bank. Inside, the letter from the bank manager confirmed that her bank account was effectively closed. They had been trying to contact me to ensure that all accounts and safe deposit boxes were cleared. When I couldn't be reached, they mailed the contents of Ms. Bremen's safe deposit box to her next of kin. I didn't have to worry about the CDs, bonds, and money Grandma Ivie had left for Brian and me. We had transferred those to another bank already.

***

That following Monday, on my first day back at work, I couldn't help but grin widely as my co-workers congratulated me on my nuptials and called me by my new name, Agent Moderze. Although I was back at the office, I wasn't ready to work; I wanted to spend more time with my new husband. I forced myself into my office and closed the door behind me.

A beep from my computer said I had a message. From my next in command, it said a shelter down on 44th had caught fire while I was on my honeymoon, just idle chit chat.

Still, I regretted the loss to the community.

Then a great idea hit me. I could open a women's shelter in Momma's name, Nancy's Home, a fitting legacy for Momma. Ottis Strut's money would rebuild the shelter that had just burned and pay the employees to run it for many years.

I needed to discuss the idea with Daimhin when I arrived home later that evening. Of course, I would have to lie how I got the money. I could tell him that I had inherited it from Grandma.

I dropped into my chair behind my desk, picked up the phone, and dialed his cell. When he picked up, I sang, "Hey, Mr. Moderze, this is Mrs. Moderze, your lovely new bride."

"That you are!" His smile sweetened his voice. "How can I help you, Mrs. Moderze?"

"You work late tonight?" He certainly had a lot to catch up on after so long away.

"No, not tonight. I want to come home to my wife and smother her in kisses."

"Great! And I would love for you to do just that. Also, I have a project that I would like to invest in, but I want to talk to you about it and get some ideas."

"Sure. I will be home no later than five-thirty. You can run this project by me then. I am always interested in my darling wife's ideas."

"I love to hear you say *my wife*! See you at home in a few hours. Thanks, babe. Love you."

"Love you too, Brea."

***

That evening at home, in my closet while undressing, I thought to give Brian a call. I had not spoken with him since the wedding. He's never visited home much, always unavailable, which had me thinking again about the murders. I wanted so badly to ask him to confirm what I knew in my heart, since no one else knew about Momma's journal, but I had promised myself to let it go because everyone was happy.

I picked up the receiver and dialed his cell number. The phone rang once, twice, three times, and then he picked up. "Hey, little brother. We're back home. Had an awesome honeymoon. I am in love, Bri, and I am married! Can you believe it?"

"I am so happy for you, Brea," he replied. "Grandma Ivie and Momma would be so happy too."

"Yeah, finally some happiness for Momma after a life of pain and sorrows." The words oozed from my mouth sad and slow. "Have you ever thought about our father, Brian?" I don't know why I asked that question.

"May he burn in hell the way he burned at the motel," replied Brian in a grave voice.

It took a while before I could properly process what I heard. When it set in properly, the phone slipped out of my hand, and I threw my head back into the wall. My eyes filled up and my lips quivered. The tears dropped. I lay on the closet floor, my body shaking violently with sobs of anguish.

All those years I had been wondering about the death of my father, but I would never thought Brian was capable of such a thing. I was on the floor, curled into a ball, when I heard Daimhin approach. I hurriedly sat up and wiped my eyes.

Daimhin kneeled beside me. "What's wrong? Are you okay?"

I shook my head. "Yes, I am, just missing Brian."

Daimhin kept his arms wrapped around me and held me close. "I'm here now to take care of you, and I am sure that Brian would approve." As I leaned toward Daimhin, he wiped a lone tear away with his finger. "I love you, Brea."

I smiled and kissed him on the cheek. "I love you too."

# ACKNOWLEDGMENTS

Everyday writing is hard enough. Writing a story you have conjured in your mind is even harder. I could not have completed this book without the help of so many others. Many thanks to all of those who worked with me on the story. Thank you for patience, time and understanding. Much credit to them for such magnificent work—credit me with all the rest.

My editor, Leigh Hogan (leigh.hogan.editing@gmail.com), You are the best. I cannot thank you enough for the encouragement, the straight forwardness. Pushing me to be my best, you would not let me give up on the story or give up on me.

My proofreader, Denise Fortowsky (dfortowsky@gmail.com), thank you for working with me.

Naeem Khan (Fiverr.com) my cover designer, thank you so much for your kindness and patience. Always a pleasure.

Kimolisa thank you for such great formatting, making the pages look fly.

As always, I acknowledge my Lord and Savior for everything big and small.

Last but never least, I credit my family. None of my stories would have been written without you. You inspire me. And I love you all dearly.

# ABOUT THE AUTHOR

*Do one thing every day that scares you. —*
Eleanor Roosevelt

just Deirdre was born in New Orleans, Louisiana, and grew up in Kansas City. Since then, she moved around until finally settling in Alabama. She has been in a long-distance relationship with her significant other for twenty years. Deirdre has three adult children, four grandchildren, and one grand dog who all live in Georgia.

Class of 1981 graduate from FL Schlagle High, Deirdre was a single parent and worked hard to support her family. At the age of forty, she attended Strayer University, where she obtained a master's degree in business administration. Deirdre is a government employee by day, but in her spare time, her creative writing alter ego, Petite Breaux, takes center stage.

Petite Breaux has written a memoir *Slightly Bruised and a Little Broken*, a short story *The Whispering of My Heart*, and children's book *Fun with Grandma*. She has recently released several short stories and a suspense novel. She is currently working on a novel, Kallista: The Forbidden One, to be released September 2019 under the name **just Deirdre**.

When she gets the time, Deirdre enjoys exercising at her local gym. She loves watching TV and goes to the theater whenever a movie grabs her attention. She also reads daily and is learning meditation for rejuvenation of the soul.

Deirdre also enjoys getting away from it all on vacation, with cruising as her favorite pastime. She has plans to live her best life to the max and has done some of the things that scare her like ziplining and parasailing. She also plans to do a skydive one day.

In the future, Deirdre wants to spend time with her family, travel, and author books that will entertain across generations.

## You can contact just Deirdre or follow her at:

Website: https://www.petitebreaux.com
Email: petitebreaux@yahoo.com
Twitter: https://twitter.com/AuthorPetiteB
Facebook: https://www.facebook.com/petitebreaux

# PLEASE REVIEW

I hope you enjoyed reading The Journal: The Nancy Bremen Story as much as I enjoyed writing it. Of course, I would appreciate a brief review on Amazon, Goodreads, or your favorite online book retailer. Just one line could make a difference as reviews are crucial for authors to be successful, particularly us indie authors.

Here is a special reader preview of my 2020 new release **Kallista, The Forbidden One**. Will be available in Ebook, paperback and hardback. Get your copy and please leave a review.

# 1 | KALLISTA

*2018 Denver Colorado*

KALLISTA TURNED AND walked out of the house with Blake following closely behind. She wouldn't take her prize under the watchful eyes of all the girls at the party. She swayed her hips seductively sensing the thumping sound of his heart. He desired her, and there was a triumphant feeling to that. His arousal and heightened hormones climaxed her sexuality. It would be a sweet conquest.

A grove of trees just outside the house and toward the backyard was the ideal place for a kill, but first she would have a great deal of fun with his body. Kallista laughed at his excited thoughts. He thought about how he'd never had sex with an older woman and the envy on his buddies' faces when he relayed the experience to them.

He was too engrossed by the swaying motion of her hips and the mounds of her breasts to care about where they were headed. He had just one thing on his mind: burying himself in her gorgeous body. Kallista thought he had quite an imagination, picturing all the different sexual positions he hoped to try out.

"We're here," she said, rousing him from his thoughts.

It was a small clearing, twenty feet of open ground surrounded by a circle of trees, illuminated by the moon. He smiled and she read his mind—he planned to put that beautiful woman's back to a tree and give her the best sex of her life.

In a forceful jerk, he pulled her in close. She liked it rough, so she welcomed his aggressiveness. Kallista gave him an amused look when he pushed her against the closest tree.

"So, what would you like me to do to you?" he asked.

"Lots of nasty things," Kallista said, chuckling.

"Oh, naughty girl, huh? I like it." He paused. "Wait, why are your eyes like that?" He took half a step back.

"Um, they change color when I get excited... I mean, really excited. You must be doing something right," she said, pulling him back closer.

With Kallista's back against the tree, he began to kiss her neck and fondle her breasts with total abandon. He moved his mouth to her chest and his hand to her crotch. The delicious richness of her soft moans washed over him. She buried his other hand in her hair, and he responded by pulling her even closer.

"Enough foreplay. Let's fuck," Blake said.

A look of delight played out on her face. She fixed her now blood-orange eyes on Blake and worked her compulsion. While hearing him scream would be exciting, she would have to pass this time given the circumstances. She needed him willing and pliant, even in the throes of pain.

Before he could blink, she switched positions and pushed him against the tree.

Nervous and unsettled, his eyes opened wide as he stared at her.

Kallista sneered at him and took his lower lip between her mouth. As she held him close, she felt a sizeable erection against her thigh. She found it intriguing and decided it was pointless letting that entire "gift" go to waste. She went on her knees and freed his cock from the constriction of his jeans.

"Oh, yeah! Get that dick!" he said in an exaggerated whisper.

She swaddled her mouth around his cock and sighed blissfully as the first bit of pre-cum cocktail hit her tongue. It was the first time she had her mouth around a man's penis, and she felt utterly exhilarated. All she'd ever known were the gratification that comes with quenching the thirst for blood.

She had heard thoughts and the talk of oral sex, in nightclubs and bars, but she'd never experienced it. Kallista believed nothing could feel more powerful and exciting than draining someone of their blood and their mortality.

But, strangely enough, she seemed to know exactly where to lick and suck to get what she wanted. Sucking dick was as invigorating as drinking blood, which she did her entire life. Until now.

Kallista watched as his eyes rolled to the back of his head. The rapture was intense. Perhaps knowing nothing about her other than her first name made it exciting, the novelty and spontaneity of it all. Nonetheless, she had him bound in a cloud of ecstasy, the likes of which he'd never felt before.

"Oh, God! Oh my God! You're amazing!" he garbled, his body tensing.

Kallista, also captivated by the arousing experience, heard his voice, but it sounded like she was miles away from him. A slight breeze blew her hair as she continued licking and sucking every inch of his shaft. Her body was alive, her breathing was erratic. It was different. She reached a high unlike any she'd ever felt, and when he came, semen flowed down her throat and her cells regenerated. The pinnacle of any ordeal she ever received.

"Whoa! Wait a minute! You're glowing!" he said, after the post-coital euphoria subsided.

"I feel amazing," Kallista responded, taking a pause and returning to her feet. She reveled in the glow that radiated from her body—stroking the smoothness of her skin, flipping her hands over, relishing her newfound youthfulness.  Her skin, which worried her moments ago, radiated as if she were a newborn.

She threw her head back and let out a low but wicked laugh. Elated, her thirst more commanding than ever, Kallista moved like the wind, her speed like lightning. One moment she was right in front of him, and the next second, she was on him like a wild animal. He couldn't have seen her coming. There was no time to protest; the fear was instantaneous, and fright fluttered in his chest.

Terror surged within him, her beautiful Nordic white hair he admired moments ago looked like fire—a bonfire. She pinned him down, her fangs buried deep in his neck. Kallista drank voraciously. The blood was thick and delicious, exactly what she needed after the blissfulness from his cum. She felt a marriage of climactic feelings; it was amazing, animalistic, and primal, and she loved every bit of it. Blake whimpered in pain, and she giggled. His pain brought her pleasure. She drank to fill and did not stop until he took his last breath.

Getting back on her feet, a small trail of blood ran down her lips toward her chin, she licked it off with relish. Her skin still glowed under the bright moonlight. Her fear of aging was gone. She'd discovered her real fountain of youth.

"I will live forever," she said, her voice resonating through the night. Music still blared from the fraternity house, but her surroundings were serene. She looked down at the young man's body. "I will never forget you. One never forgets the first practice." She smiled victoriously as she tiptoed over the body and walked away.

*One Hour Earlier*

The murky expanse became darker as the humid summer night went on. The sunrays had long since disappeared over the horizon, replaced by thousands of stars. A light breeze rustled the leaves as Kallista looked through the tree branches. Now, the night was dark, and the moon was nowhere to be found.

Kallista heard a party in the distance. She glanced down at her glittering dress. It ended mid-thigh—a perfect outfit for an uninvited party guest. With a raised eyebrow and a deep-seated chuckle, she thought about how women dresses had evolved from the time she was a girl. That said, Kallista never cared for anyone's opinion, nor did she follow the rules of attire—that was all too boring, and she didn't abide by such nonsense.

Walking into the Boulder Colorado Frat house, she took in the whole scene. She owned the room. Bodies rocked to the music, and the alcohol flowed freely. It was exactly as she expected: young men and women in various stages of fornication, bodies intertwined on the dance floor and in dark corners. Kallista could smell the hormones all over the place. She closed her eyes, took a deep breath, and the sexual scent assailed her system, arousing her senses. Kallista's body throbbed with sensation from within. It would be an exciting night.

After a few seconds, all eyes at the party were fixated on her. She had no care in the world to give. She could see the guys checking her out and the young women glancing furtively as they whispered.

"Who is she!? What is she doing here?

"Does anyone know her? Who invited her?"

"Look at her skin, flawless as smooth cream. She is gorgeous."

She was an exquisite woman, with tantalizing silver eyes and a curvaceous body that men would go to war for. Kallista never had to wonder what anyone was thinking. Besides her incredible beauty, she had the ability of telepathy and could plant ideas and thoughts in the minds of others.

No corner of the house was safe from the music's roar. They ran amok, those human children, frolicking anywhere they could. Free rein and it was plain they loved the way it felt. Freedom, Kallista recognized, could be as addictive as a drug, a stage she had already gone past. She went through it a long time ago, not long after she left the coven.

She touched the tip of her tongue to her fangs, and her mouth watered. All she wanted was to eat. It had been a long time since she had blood—nineteen hours, to be exact—and it was time to sate her hunger. A fleeting sense of pity ran through her mind for her next victim, whoever it would be. He or she wouldn't survive the night.

Perplexed, she took a quick glimpse in the massive mirror in the foyer, taking in her albino skin and the faint wrinkles around the eyes. Something about her was changing. For a ninety-five-year-old human, it was expected, but she was a hybrid vampire with the youthfulness of a thirty-year-old; she should not be aging. It was not what she wanted. However, she knew how it worked. She was half-human, and that tainted part of her blood caused her cells to gradually degenerate. Her mother remained the same since her vampire birthing, which was three hundred years ago—or so she liked to brag.

Kallista chased the thought from her mind and focused on the task ahead. Her throat parched with a dry burning sensation, to the extent she already imagined the flow of thick human blood streaming down it and the relief it would bring. It was bound to be glorious; there was nothing more satisfying than feeding after hours of going without feeding.

The party rocked—bottles of alcohol were all over the place, and even more cigarettes. Kallista hated nicotine; its pungent smell reduced the sweetness of human blood. It was easy to spot a smoker from the stale scent coming from beneath their skin, and she was not interested in any of them.

Kallista smiled to herself as she watched the young college students do all the silly things children do—dissolving in laughter, touching their bodies, lacing their fingers, and screaming for no reason.

Then a blue-eyed, ash-blond young man took her out of her fixation with his unabashed and lustful stare. She had a thing for attractive faces, so she went along with it. Something was exciting about toying with food before eating it.

She pulled her thoughts away from every other person in the room and focused on the young man who stared rather bawdy at her. He stood with his back against the wall, one hand in a pocket and the other holding a bottle of beer. His jeans were deliberately worn but clean, and they fit him well, adding to his lustful demeanor. Her lips parted as her eyes traveled along the lines of his lean body. He was ideal for her. She could see his muscles rippling under the tight outline of his T-shirt, and she instantly knew how the encounter would end. She could feel his body temperature rise from across the room.

Kallista could tell the young man considered himself an alpha male, one of the most popular guys on campus all the girls wanted. Those used to getting all the attention and would discard those who did not meet his standard.

Still observing him, she watched him slowly exhale as his eyes moved from her lips to her breasts, then to her hips, and back up to her lips. She wanted him to desire her with a ferocity that scared him. She wanted him to feel her soft lips against his—it would be the most ridiculous and exciting thing she had ever encountered.

She bit her lower lip subtly, but the way his body responded was not subtle. In no time, he stood upright and headed toward her.

"You are so damn beautiful... but I'm sure you knew that," he said. Kallista liked his smoothness and amused him with a side smile. "It must be my lucky night. I'm Blake," he added.

"It is your night," she said playfully. "*Come with me,*" she said using compulsion—without sound, just voices in his head. That was all it took for him to salivate after her, anticipating the moment.

"I'd follow you anywhere," he said with a dazed expression.

"Yes, you will."